THE SCIENTIFIC ADVENTURES OF THE SUGIMORI SISTERS

BRIGID COLLINS

Frosty Owl
Publishing

The Scientific Adventures of the Sugimori Sisters

Cover design © 2025 Brigid Collins

Frosty Owl Publishing

Paperback
ISBN: 979-8-89728-018-6

 Created with Vellum

OTHER BOOKS BY BRIGID COLLINS

THE SONGBIRD RIVER CHRONICLES SERIES
Singer
The Southern Dragon
The Fount of Magic
The Dark Ways

WINTER'S CONSORT
A Prisoner to Spring
An Ally in Summer
An Enemy by Autumn
A Protector over Winter

THE CLOCKWORK KINGDOM SAGA
Clockwork Princess

FAIRIES AND FASTBALLS (With Ron Collins)
Home Run Enchanted
Curveball Cursed
Outfield Magicked

THE SUGIMORI SISTERS SERIES
The Scientific Adventures of the Sugimori Sisters
Further Scientific Mayhem! With the Sugimori Sisters
The Holiday Experiment Files of the Sugimori Sisters

NOVELLAS
Thorn and Thimble

SHORT FICTION
Three Tales of Faeries
Three Tales of Powers
Three Tales of Monsters
Three Tales of Nightmares

Acknowledgments

Thank you to my father for being my guinea pig on these stories, and to my mother for making them shine with perfect grammar and punctuation. Any remaining errors are my own.

Thank you to my friends Michael, Rob, Alex, and Clarence for all the lunches spent talking and commiserating about the business of writing.

ONE

The Interplanetary Concept Clash

Ellen Sugimori fought to keep the heat of shame from showing on her face. If her mom had *tried* to embarrass her in front of the entire sixth-grade class, she couldn't have done a more effective job. Since the move from Lansing, Ellen was a new student this year. She didn't need her mom adding to her status of *weird*.

Ellen watched her mom take her tiny, shuffling steps out of the classroom and braced herself for the slithering snickers she knew her classmates had been holding back throughout the presentation.

Ellen should have said no two weeks ago when her history teacher had asked her to invite her mom to do a presentation on the Japanese tea ceremony for the class.

"But my mom doesn't speak English," Ellen had protested, keeping her voice low so the other students wouldn't hear.

"You can translate for her. Your classmates will be impressed that you speak Japanese as well as English."

Ellen knew they wouldn't. Worse, they would know that her mom wasn't like theirs; she wasn't a normal American mom who made peanut butter and jelly sandwiches for her lunch or drove her to soccer practice after school. They would know that her mom was stupid and weird.

And none of the other kids would be impressed with her mom's choice of clothes.

Why, oh, *why* had her mom come to school in a *kimono*?

As the other kids chattered, Ellen picked up the tea cups and leftover matcha powder. Ellen took the cups to the sink in the back of the classroom to wash them before shoving them into her backpack.

Her mouth was dry from the translating and from standing by the chalkboard for so long, where the air was full of the tasteless white dust. But she didn't ask to go get a drink.

Ellen didn't dare look at any of the other kids for the rest of the day. She couldn't bear to see their teasing faces, so she kept her eyes forward and sat on her hands so she wouldn't accidentally raise them to answer questions.

Instead, Ellen spent the whole class stewing over the culture project she had to do for Japanese school next week. She had to go every Saturday to study her Japanese heritage and language, as if she didn't get enough of that at home. She still hadn't decided what to do for the project since everything she thought of sounded boring and irrelevant. They didn't live in Japan, after all. They lived in Detroit.

People in Detroit didn't do things like the tea ceremony or flower arranging.

When the final bell rang, Ellen pushed her chair back so fast it screeched against the floor. Grabbing up her backpack and swinging it over her shoulder, Ellen dashed out the door ahead of everyone else.

The tea cups clinked against each other as she fast-walked out of the building. Ellen heard them even over the screams and laughs of other students pouring out into the freedom of the afternoon.

Outside, she slowed down and took a deep breath. Summer vacation was almost here, and Ellen thought the neighborhood smelled *green*. Like leaves and sunshine.

She kicked at pebbles on the sidewalk as she walked to her house three blocks away. The fact that they lived so close to school made her nervous, just thinking about how easy it would be for one of her friends to find out what her family was really like.

Ellen snorted. Not so much of an issue anymore, was it?

And her mom had called her Eriko! How many times did she have to tell her she wanted to be called Ellen? The name was much more elegant and grown-up. Eriko sounded like a little kid's name.

Not to mention her friends couldn't pronounce it very well.

"Mom's lived in America for thirteen years," Ellen mumbled. "Why hasn't she learned to speak English yet? It's not hard."

Nobody was around to answer her, so Ellen just slouched the rest of the way home.

She reached their driveway at house number 544 and walked up it, careful not to step on any cracks. No weeds poked up from them, thanks to her dad's meticulous yard work every weekend. Their potted flowers added splashes of red and pink to the front walk and porch, all done in a traditional Japanese fashion.

Little Sister has been scribbling on the driveway again, she noticed. Addition and subtraction problems covered the cracked concrete, and dotted lines connected circles like a path on a treasure map.

As if the thought were a magic conjuration, Risako appeared from the back yard. "What took you so long?"

Ellen rolled her eyes. "You first-graders get out an hour earlier than the sixth-graders do."

"Oh, right. Well, do you want to come to Saturn with me?"

"Saturn?"

"I just finished my spaceship!"

Ellen pictured the cardboard and plastic monstrosity that had taken up the corner of the back yard for the past week. "Oh. Okay, I guess I can play with you for a little while."

The longer she could delay going inside and seeing her mom, the better.

Ellen followed Little Sister around the house, her backpack clinking with every step.

She had to admit, Little Sister's construction was impressive. Any six-year-old could throw slabs of cardboard together and claim it was a spaceship, but Little Sister's creation actually looked like a space-worthy vessel.

Paper towel tubes were bunched together with rubber bands and glued to the sides to be thrusters. The front was a pointed nose cone. Properly curved cardboard fins jutted out of the top and sides. The garden hose curled around from place to place. She even had the clear plastic lid from their toy box as the windshield.

"You sit in the co-pilot's seat, Ellen," Little Sister directed, lifting the toy box lid and clambering into the other side.

Ellen held up the lid and swung her legs into the seat. She put her backpack at her feet.

Inside, it smelled like cut paper and crayons. Little Sister had drawn a control panel at the front with buttons labeled in both English and Japanese. The seats were just big, black rectangles on the floor and back wall of the cockpit.

"Okay, I'm ready for lift-off," Ellen said.

"It'll take a minute," Little Sister said, poking at some of the drawn buttons. "It runs on green energy, so it needs to collect enough green from the grass first."

"Green energy?" Ellen asked.

"We're learning about it in school this week. Mrs. Carter says green energy is better for the planet, so I made my spaceship run on it."

Ellen's lips quirked up, but she didn't say anything. Why couldn't their spaceship be powered by the color green?

"Okay, we're ready," Little Sister said. "Hold on tight."

"Okay." Ellen leaned forward to put her hands on the control panel.

The thrusters fired up, and Ellen flew backward against her black crayon seat as the ship zoomed into the air.

"Ahh! What's going on?!"

Little Sister looked over at her. "We're going to Saturn, dummy. I told you to hold on."

"It's pretend! What did you *do*?" How could Little Sister just pilot her cardboard spaceship like it flew through the air every day?

Little Sister didn't answer her question, too focused on propelling them through the turbulence of the atmosphere.

Higher and higher they flew, and Ellen held her breath. Her ears popped.

Weren't airplanes pressurized so people's heads wouldn't explode or something? She didn't want her head to explode, and she definitely didn't want to get Little Sister's brains splattered all over her school clothes. Mom would throw a fit.

The cardboard and plastic rattled all around them as air buffeted the ship. Ellen scrabbled her fingers around the cockpit, searching for something to hold onto. They flew faster and faster, up and up, and the rushing wind grew louder and louder.

The shaking stopped. They smoothed out and shot away from planet Earth and into the inky, star-speckled darkness of space.

Ellen twisted in her seat, trying to look back towards home, but she couldn't manage it.

"I should have put a window in the back," Little Sister admitted.

Ellen settled back in her seat, letting out a shaky breath. "How long until we reach Saturn?"

Little Sister poked at some of the crayon squares and squinted at the big one in the middle. Ellen realized that it was supposed to be a display screen, but nothing appeared on it.

It was just a square drawn on cardboard, after all.

"Probably only twenty minutes," Little Sister said with a shrug. "Green energy is very efficient."

"Watch out!" Ellen screamed.

The Moon loomed before them through the plastic toy box lid, so bright it was blinding.

They were headed for a collision!

Little Sister wrestled with the controls. The spaceship turned to the right, but the Moon still got closer and closer.

"We need more speed!" Ellen shouted. "Full power on the thrusters!"

She jabbed at the square labeled THRUSTERS スラスタ, and the ship lurched. They pulled away to the right, just skimming a few feet above the surface of the Moon.

Ellen watched the craters whizz by, trying not to think about how close they'd just come to becoming a crater themselves.

"That was too close, Little Sister," Ellen said, slumping back in her seat. "You have to be a responsible driver."

Little Sister giggled. "You sound like mom."

"I do not."

"Do, too."

"Mom doesn't know the word 'responsible,' and she sounds stupid when she tries to say 'drive.' *Doraibuuuuu*." Ellen extended the last syllable, trying to make Little Sister laugh.

Little Sister did laugh. "Yeah, but she says the same things in Japanese. Be responsible, do your homework, study Kanji! I wish we didn't have to go to Japanese School on Saturdays."

Ellen sighed. "Me, too." Normal American kids didn't have to go to Japanese School.

It wasn't that she didn't *like* her Japanese heritage. Anime was cool, and she had a whole collection of manga. Some of the video games were fun, when she could convince dad to buy them for her. But the tea ceremony was boring, and calligraphy and Kanji sucked. She worried about her culture project again.

She sighed once more, then sniffed.

"I smell burning paper," she said.

"Oh, no," Little Sister moaned. She poked at the buttons and squinted at the blank display. "The brush with the Moon damaged the fuel tank. We're running on fumes!"

"Green has fumes?" Ellen asked.

But there was no time to question it. The sputtering, jerking motion of the ship shook the left thruster loose, and it sent them spinning.

Little Sister and Ellen grappled with the controls to pull themselves into a straight path. When they reached a semi-steady trajectory, a bright plane of rusty red filled their view.

"Mars!" Little Sister squealed.

"We're gonna crash!"

They hurtled through the atmosphere of the red planet.

Sweat rolled down Ellen's face and back as their entry heated up the cockpit. The smell of burning paper surrounded her, and she squinched her eyes closed and pressed her lips together to keep from screaming.

A hard jolt and a loud ripple of crumpling cardboard signified their arrival.

For having crash-landed on Mars, the spaceship didn't look too bad. The nose was stuck in the red dirt and crunched up, and one thruster dangled by a thin strip of masking tape, but otherwise, it looked as flight-worthy as it ever had.

Little Sister tugged on the back to pull it out of the dirt. The garden hose flopped amongst the rocks, and Little Sister groaned.

"The fuel tank's been completely drained," she said. "I can fix the hole, but we need to find more green stuff to get home."

Ellen glanced around. "But we're on Mars. There's no green here."

Little Sister frowned at the back of the ship, rubbing her chin the way dad did when he was trying to solve a problem.

"I could make an adaptor," she mumbled. "Something to let the ship run on red. But I would need some construction paper and red and green building bricks."

Ellen's heart sank and rolled around in her tummy. "I don't think we'll find any of those here."

"Then we've got to look for them."

Ellen wrapped her arms around herself and followed Little Sister away from the ship. She glanced back at it, trying to imagine how any of this could have happened.

A reddish-brown smudge streaked across the horizon to their

left, and Ellen worried about Mars's famous dust storms. She didn't want to get caught in one. The dust rose in puffs around her feet, and the wind dragged it across the ground. It pushed at Ellen's back with its dry chill, urging her to catch up with Little Sister.

Far ahead of her, Little Sister stopped and pointed down. "A rover! Ellen, look."

Ellen came up beside her at the edge of a short drop. They were on top of a plateau. At the bottom, just as Little Sister said, a Mars rover sat motionless.

She thought it looked like a big bird with a long neck and six legs. Maybe a weird dragon? But not a Japanese dragon, because the solar panels looked like wings.

"Great! Maybe we can contact NASA and get them to get us home," she said. She inched herself over the edge and slid down it in a shower of rocks and red dust.

"Hello?" she said to the silent rover. "Uh, Houston?"

Little Sister came over to the rover, brushing dust from her pants. She peered at the machine, and swept a hand over the flat table of dusty solar panels.

"I think it's sleeping, or broken," she said. "Look, it's stuck in the dirt here."

Ellen looked at the rover's wheels. Dirt had piled up around them, rendering the machine immobile. "Can we dig it out and get it running again?"

Little Sister shrugged. "Let's try."

They both got on their hands and knees, scooping the dirt away from the wheels until some of them were unburied.

Little Sister sat back and wiped her hand over her forehead, smearing red dirt across her face. "I don't know if we can get it out. Let me see if I can get it to turn on."

Little Sister clambered up onto one of the solar panel wings and tapped on the camera.

"Be careful you don't fall off," Ellen said as a strong gust of wind whipped around the plateau.

The landscape was nothing like home. No trees or grass grew, no water flowed. Having lived in a flat part of Michigan all her life, Ellen found all these hills unsettling. The red everywhere made her think the place should be blazing hot, but she shivered every time the wind whistled by. If it was going to be cold, there ought to at least be some snow to play in.

Ellen wanted to go home, where she knew how to interact with her environment.

"Agh, I can't do anything without materials!" Little Sister lamented. She leapt off of the solar panels and landed in the dust with a *flump*. "If I had some more cardboard and some pipe cleaners, I could get it working again."

"Is there anything green on it?" Ellen asked. If they could at least get some fuel for their ship, the rover wouldn't be a total dud.

"Maybe underneath? Or inside. Computer chips are green, right?"

Ellen and Little Sister knelt back in the dirt and wriggled beneath the rover's belly.

Ellen ran her finger over a seam in the body. "Let's get this open."

"Halt!"

Ellen and Little Sister both gasped and jumped. Ellen bumped her head against the rover.

From her spot on the ground, she saw four metallic legs marching through the dust and rocks towards them. Each leg was capped with a flat, round foot, which pivoted to conform to the rocky ground.

The metal legs stopped just by the rover, and a whirr of machinery accompanied the appearance of a pair of binocular-like eyes. The eyes scanned over the two of them on the end of a long, snaky metal cord.

"Come away from the silent watcher, Earthlings."

Ellen and Little Sister hurried to obey. Before them stood a four-legged, two-armed robot. The binocular eyes snapped into place above a square metal speaker.

"Are you a rover?" Ellen asked.

The robot rotated its eyes and speaker around the pole that made up its body. "I am a grave keeper. Why have you come to our resting place, Earthlings?"

"We didn't mean to," said Little Sister. "We were going to Saturn, but we crash-landed here. We're out of fuel. Do you have any green stuff?"

"Grrreeeeen?" the grave keeper repeated, lengthening the word like he didn't understand how to pronounce it.

"Green, like grass or trees or Oscar the Grouch?" Little Sister pressed.

The grave keeper rotated its eyes again. "Are you a new version of the silent watcher? We spoke with it before it died, but it did not understand our concept of 'two.' You have a new concept that I do not understand, this grrreeeeen. My analysis shows that this may be blasphemy, and I should take you in."

"Wait, what?" Ellen said.

The grave keeper did not elaborate but reached out with its two arms faster than Ellen could blink. It picked both of them up and hoisted them over its binocular eyes.

"Hey!" Ellen yelled, kicking her legs and pulling on the arms with her hands. "Put us down."

The grave keeper ignored them and walked away from the rover. Its metal feet crunched over the rocks. "I will take you down to City 542 and show you to the Server. It will judge this grrreeeeen, and you."

~

The grave keeper took them to an underground city made of red and brown buildings. The streetlamps shone orange over the pink stone of the roads, where large robots with thick wheels trundled from place to place.

Other types of robots crawled along the sidewalks or hopped across the street. A few tiny ones even flew through the air with rotating helicopter blades.

All of them spoke to each other in a strange, beeping and clicking language of computer sounds.

"What are they saying?" Little Sister asked as two robots swiveled their eyes to watch them pass.

"You don't know?" asked the grave keeper. "That is embarrassing. Our language is simple. They are preparing for our Festival of Calculations tomorrow. Your arrival interrupts our work."

Ellen glanced up at a long yellow banner stretching between two buildings and tried to make out the words on it.

The grave keeper carried them into a large brown building lit with red light bulbs.

A computer hum vibrated down the long corridor, and Ellen stared at the bundles of cables and pipes running along the walls. The grave keeper's four feet clopped like a horse's hooves on the sheet metal floor plates.

They passed under a large ventilating fan. Ellen peered up into it and thought she could see a tiny speck of brown Martian sky far above her. The *whump-whump* of the blades drowned out any sound of outside, though.

Even with the fan, Ellen was sweating from the heat of the machines. Her school clothes stuck to her skin, and beads of moisture collected on her face. She struggled to wipe at them in her awkward position above the grave keeper's head.

The corridor widened, and they arrived at a large doorway. The grave keeper stepped through it without pausing and walked to the center of the room.

Then it brought its arms down and dropped the two girls onto the floor.

"Server, I found two Earthlings on the surface, desecrating the remains of both our dead and the silent watcher. They speak of a concept called grreeeen, which I calculate may be blasphemy."

Ellen rubbed at her elbow where she'd bashed it against the floor and stared at her surroundings.

The walls of the room flared with tiny lights. They blinked in patterns she couldn't understand. Cables crisscrossed the walls and the floor. The whole place smelled hot and sterile, without a speck of dust in it.

The computer hum increased, and Ellen slid towards Little Sister. Whatever was going to happen, she wouldn't let it hurt her sister.

"Earthlings, *hmmm*? And a blasphemous concept. The penalty for blasphemy is imprisonment until your circuits rust over."

The deep voice came from every direction at once, and Ellen hunched over Little Sister, feeling like a cornered animal.

Little Sister shifted to sit cross-legged. "We don't have any circuits, we're humans. Does that mean we'll be imprisoned forever?"

"Risako!" Ellen hissed.

The deep voice surrounded them again, and Ellen noticed that a number of speakers were set into the walls to create a stereo effect.

"You will be imprisoned for an appropriate time if you are guilty of blasphemy. Tell us more about this grreeeen."

Little Sister huffed a tired sigh. "Like I told the grave keeper, green is like grass or trees or Oscar the Grouch. It's the fuel our ship runs on. If I could just borrow some construction paper and some red and green building bricks, I can fix our ship and get us back home. The construction paper can be any color, whatever you have is fine."

"Construction paper and building bricks?" the server asked. "We do not have such building materials. And your request does not answer the question of grreeeeen. If you cannot properly explain it, you will be imprisoned."

Little Sister thumped her fists on the floor. "How can you not know what green is? It's a color just like all the others. Some apples are green, and some grapes."

The server whirred in all the walls.

The grave keeper stepped forward. "My own blasphemy calculations are rising. I do not know any of the things this Earthling mentions. Shall we imprison them for however long it takes their circuits to rust?"

"Computer chips!" Little Sister screamed. "Ellen and I were trying to get at the green chips inside the rover when you found us. Surely you know what computer chips are!"

The server rumbled, and the lights quickened their blinking. The heat rose to a blazing level of discomfort. Ellen heard the fan in the hallway rev up.

"You would disassemble one who has come to its final rest in the resting place of the surface? You must be some sort of virus to perform such foul surgeries. Lock them up!"

A siren sounded through the building, and the tromping of boots on steel floor reverberated into the server's room. Ellen and Little Sister cowered on the floor while three sentry robots marched in. They each held some sort of silver gun in their three-fingered hands, and the soles of their feet were covered with rubber grips like tires.

"Come with us, do not resist," said the one in the lead. Its voice was monotonous.

It reached out to grasp Little Sister by her shirt.

"Wait!" Ellen cried. "Green is like *matcha*. I forgot I had it in my backpack left over from the tea ceremony. We don't need building bricks or anything to get home."

She looked around the room, unsure where the server's eyes were. "Is that acceptable? We'll go home and never come back to bother you about green stuff again."

The server hummed. "A ceremony we understand. We will have one here tomorrow. But this teeee, I cannot calculate. Is this more blasphemy?"

Ellen stomped her foot and screamed. "How about this? You all come with us back to our ship, where I'll show you the tea ceremony. You'll see what green is, and then we can go home."

If the server suggested that demonstrations were blasphemy, she would do something drastic, like eat her shoes.

After a long moment of whirring and blinking lights, the server delivered its verdict.

"My guards and the grave keeper will go with you to see this teeee ceremony and grreeeeen. They will then decide what percentage of your words is blasphemy and whether you should be locked up until your circuits rust."

Ellen's whoop of victory stopped in her throat when the guards clamped their three-fingered hands around her arms and marched her and Little Sister back down the corridor.

At least they were headed back to the ship, where they could attempt an escape plan.

Out in the cold, red dust fields again, Ellen and Little Sister trudged before their robot captors. The plateau and the ship lay just before them, blurred by the dusty wind.

They passed by the old rover, and Little Sister sighed.

"It would be so great to get that thing working again."

Ellen shrugged and clambered up the side of the plateau. When she reached the top, she stretched a hand out to Little Sister.

The four robots came up as well, the grave keeper moving faster than the guards with his specialized feet.

"Show us this grreeeen teeee ceremony, Earthlings," said the lead guard once everyone had reached the top. It waved its silver gun at the wreck of their spaceship.

Ellen bit her lip at the sight of the wreckage. "Do you think you can fix the thruster and the fuel tank?" she asked Little Sister, keeping her voice low.

Little Sister circled the ship and nodded.

"Okay," Ellen said. "I'll get the stuff from my backpack, and you work on that."

She fumbled with the toy box lid and tugged her backpack out from the co-pilot's seat. It scraped against the cardboard side some, but she got it up and slung over her shoulder with a grunt.

The tea cups clinked as she walked back to where the robots waited.

"I'll have to do a short version of the ceremony," Ellen explained as she dug the tea items out. "We don't have a hanging scroll, or any flower arrangements, and my classmates already ate all the sweets you're supposed to serve. But we've got enough matcha powder to make the tea."

The robots craned over her as she arranged the tea bowl, the whisk, and the tea scoop with the container of powder on the flattest part of the ground she could find. Luckily, Ellen had some water left in her bottle she could use to make the tea. She tried to ignore their curious stares, but she couldn't help feeling like every move she made had an impact on her ability to get herself and Little Sister out of this situation and back home.

Finally, Ellen couldn't take their hovering anymore. "You four sit down in front of me while I make the tea."

The four robots looked at one another, then followed her instructions. They sat in a perfect line, the three guards looking like they'd just come off an assembly line they were so identical. The grave keeper held itself a little less stiffly, leaning forward with its binocular eyes pushed out to get a better look.

"When will you show us grreeeeen?" it asked. Ellen thought its voice sounded breathless. Was it excited?

"Right now," Ellen said, lifting the matcha container. She pulled the lid off and tipped it over the tea bowl. She shielded the rim of the bowl from the dusty wind, not wanting to lose any of the precious powder. It would be their rocket fuel, after all.

All four of the robots made a crackling sound in their speakers, and Ellen looked up to see them reel backwards in obvious shock. Then they leaned forwards.

"It exists," said the guard leader. "The Earthlings were not lying about the grreeeeen."

"Our big brother will be pleased!" said one. The third guard nudged it with its elbow and hissed, "the server."

"So we can go home?" Ellen asked, pausing in her preparations.

"Show us the teeee, I want to see it," said the grave keeper. It snaked its binocular eyes over to peer into the tea bowl.

"Stop that," Ellen chastised, slapping the eyes away. "You're getting in the way. I'll show you the tea, so long as you promise that we can go home afterwards."

The grave keeper retracted its eyes, and the guards gave her synchronized nods.

"Once you prove that teeee is real, too, you can go. My report will inform the server of the two concepts, and the information you give us will be added to the database for the whole of robotdom to peruse."

Ellen looked into the tea bowl where the pile of green powder waited to be turned into tea. Her performance of the tea ceremony here would inform all the robots on Mars? A shiver of nerves ran down her spine, and she chewed on her lip.

The idea of the robots missing information, like the scroll and the flowers, made her uncomfortable. If Ellen was going to share a piece of her Earth culture, she wanted to share all of it. She pictured herself demonstrating the whole ceremony to a crowd of enraptured robots, and a surge of pride zinged through her.

And if she could wear a pretty kimono, that would be even better.

"Maybe... we could come back some time to show you the whole thing," she suggested. "We could show you other stuff we do on Earth, too."

"Yeah, like baseball and other colors you don't know about," Little Sister shouted from behind the ship.

The grave keeper nodded, and the guards agreed.

"We can show you some of our ceremonies, too, like the Festival of Calculations or the Energy-Saving Fair," said the grave keeper.

"Those sound like a blast!" Little Sister said.

Smiling, Ellen picked up her water bottle and the whisk and made the tea with a gusto she hadn't felt for the ceremony before.

As the robots beeped and made calculations over her tea, and when the six of them poured their cups of tea into the repaired fuel tank, she understood what her mom must have felt when she shared their culture with the kids at school.

"Mom?" Ellen cried as she rushed into the house, leaving Little Sister to go through her landing checklist with the spaceship by herself. "Kaa-san?"

"I'm in the kitchen," mom replied in Japanese. She sounded tired amidst the banging and burbling of dinner preparations. "Did you do your homework? You have Japanese School tomorrow."

"I know," Ellen said. "I was hoping you could help me with my project. I want to learn how to do the tea ceremony really well so I can show my friends after school tomorrow."

Her mom smiled. "Of course I'll help you, Eriko."

Ellen grinned and looked out the window. A yellow banner stretched across their neighbor's back yard, ready for a party.

She couldn't wait to go back to Mars.

TWO

The Time Machine Conflict

B right sunlight came through the large square windows to the left of the student desks. It glinted off the bookshelf under the window, bounced from the blue and green globe in the corner by the teacher's desk, slid past the poster of the Declaration of Independence tacked to the white wall, and fell in a big splotch on the chalkboard at the front of the classroom, turning the middle of the board lime green and highlighting the neatly written words: "History paper final draft due Friday".

Despite the fact history was not Ellen Sugimori's favorite class, excitement ran through her. The teacher would hand back their rough drafts at the end of class today, with her comments attached. Ellen couldn't wait to see how much Ms. Haley loved her paper on the Japanese tea ceremony.

While Ellen's classmates shared nervous glances, all worried about the extra work they would clearly have to do to polish *their* papers to a perfect final draft, Ellen smiled at her own genius.

Being of Japanese descent, Ellen went to Japanese school every Saturday. After an exciting adventure with Little Sister last summer, Ellen had done a project about the Japanese tea ceremony. Everyone at Japanese school had loved it, and the teacher called it the best project of the lesson.

When Ms. Haley announced the History paper two weeks ago, Ellen only had to tweak her project a little and write the presentation into a paper. It was the easiest paper Ellen had written all year, and she never even needed to step foot in the school's creepy, haunted library. She was dying to read Ms. Haley's praise.

"All right, class," Ms. Haley said, scooping up the pile of papers. "Once you've got your rough draft, you're free to go. Please read the comments carefully and work hard on your final drafts."

Ellen held her breath as Ms. Haley moved up and down the rows. *Finally,* the teacher reached her desk. Ellen grinned and reached for her paper. Ms. Haley smiled back, but in a funny way, with her lips very thin.

Ellen looked at her rough draft.

At the very top of the page, in red ink, read the words "Please do more research. This paper does not properly discuss the history involved."

Ellen's jaw dropped. She flipped through the pages to find them covered in more red notes.

By now, her classmates had filtered out into the hallway, and Ellen was alone with Ms. Haley.

"Did you have any questions for me, Ellen?" Ms. Haley asked. She smiled that thin-lipped smile again.

Ellen swallowed and turned back to the first page of her

paper. "I don't understand. Everyone at Japanese school liked this project."

"It's a very good project, Ellen, and I know you're excited about the tea ceremony," Ms. Haley said, "but you didn't include any of the history. Why don't you go down to the library and do some research? I bet you'd find that period of Japan's history fascinating."

Ellen gulped and tried to ignore how her hands trembled at the mention of the library.

Unable to speak around the burn of misery in her throat, Ellen nodded and shuffled out of the classroom, her rough draft crumpled in her hand.

Laughter echoed in the halls as Ellen trudged through the crowd of students. It was the sixth graders' lunch period, but Ellen couldn't join in with her classmates' jokes. She wasn't even hungry anymore, though at the beginning of class she'd been dreaming of the bento box her mom had packed her.

Ellen grimaced. Even thinking of the onigiri, usually her favorite Japanese food, made her stomach do flip-flops.

The route to the cafeteria carried the students past the school library, and Ellen glanced at the heavy-looking doors as she came up to them. A shiver went down her spine at the sight of their dark wood. They didn't even have the little windows all the classroom doors had.

Casting one look down to the cafeteria, Ellen sighed and squeezed her rough draft. Her lunch was ruined anyway.

The cool metal handle of the left-hand door tingled against her palm, but the door itself was not as heavy as it looked, and it swung open easily when Ellen pulled. When she stepped inside, the door closed again with a soft click. Silence descended as if the library door were some magical barrier against the noise of the sixth graders beyond it.

The air was so still and musty inside the library that Ellen thought she must be the only person here. The librarian's desk stood abandoned when she turned to look. Still, Ellen found herself tiptoeing past the desk and to the shelves.

Just because the librarian wasn't there to yell at her didn't mean she wanted anyone, or any*thing*, else to hear her. Was it her imagination, or were the dim lights flickering?

Ellen shivered and crept into the history section to search for books on Japan. She'd find her books and get out of here before the ghosts could catch her.

She was reaching for a book, her fingers about to brush the stiff spine, when she heard a sound.

A soft thump and the hiss of paper sliding on paper slithered from the shelves behind Ellen.

Ellen gasped and snatched her hand back. She turned towards the sound, keeping her back pressed against the bookshelf. If a library ghost was coming for her, she wouldn't let it jump on her from behind.

She held her breath and strained her ears, listening into the silence.

The papery sound came again. It was closer this time.

Ellen's heart pounded, and when she heard footsteps coming nearer, she couldn't stop the tiny whimper that escaped her.

The footsteps picked up at her sound. Ellen tensed to run, ready to abandon her research to save herself. What was a bad grade on a paper compared to being caught by a ghost?

But just as she leapt out from the Japanese History section, someone else came from around the other side of the shelf. The two of them collided painfully, and Ellen fell to the floor, her rough draft fluttering out of her hands.

"Owwww! Why don't you watch where you're going?" said the other person.

Ellen gasped. "Little Sister? What are you doing here?"

Sprawled beside her on the stiff, floral-patterned carpet was Risako, a scowl on her face and papers scattered around her.

"I'm doing research, what does it look like?" Risako said. She gathered her papers into a neat bundle, tapping them on the floor to straighten them out.

Ellen glanced around for the ghost she'd heard, but she soon determined that there had been no ghost. This time.

"You scared me, Little Sister," she said finally, pushing herself to her feet. "I thought you were one of the library ghosts."

Little Sister snorted. "There's no scientific evidence to say that ghosts exist. You can be scared of them if you want, but I prefer to stick to scientific fact."

Ellen rolled her eyes and kept glancing over her shoulders. She didn't see any harm in being careful.

"What are you researching?" Ellen asked, finally satisfied that no ghosts were hanging around.

Risako scowled at her notes. "I'm looking for information on Galileo's findings on the moons of Jupiter for the first-grader science fair, but the school library doesn't have the sources I need."

"What do you need to know?" Ellen asked.

"I want his thought process, what observations he made each night, what sort of materials he used to make his telescope. I don't think I'm using the right brand of paper towel tubes."

Ellen kept herself from rolling her eyes. Little Sister was smart for a first grader, but sometimes Ellen wondered if she had a firm grasp on reality.

"Sounds like you really just want to talk to him, then," Ellen said, thinking suddenly of her own research. How cool would it be to discuss the tea ceremony with an ancient Japanese emperor?

Oblivious to Ellen's daydreaming, Little Sister turned back

to the book shelves. "Well, I was hoping to have my time machine out of the prototype stage before testing it, but I might have to risk it if I can't find what I need for my science project."

Ellen snapped out of her thoughts of *kimono* and *samurai* and whirled to follow Little Sister. "A time machine? I thought you were getting your spaceship ready for another flight?" Ellen knew she had seen Little Sister tinkering around her cardboard monstrosity in the back yard last weekend. Ellen still couldn't believe it had actually taken them to Mars.

"Oh, I am," Little Sister said, digging around in her backpack. "The time machine is a side project. I'm trying to keep this machine compact."

She held out her favorite yellow wristwatch. A bundle of red and blue pipe cleaners was tangled around the band on either side of the face, and a small cardboard circle hung on the end of one pipe cleaner. Ellen saw scribbles in black crayon on the circle, but she couldn't make out what they might mean.

Ellen looked up to meet Little Sister's gaze. "That's a time machine?"

"Like I said, it's a prototype."

"But it can take us back in time?"

Little Sister fiddled with the arrangement of the pipe cleaners and twisted the dial on the side of the watch. "It can, but it's only strong enough right now for one trip and the return." Little Sister sighed. "I planned to test it out by going back to two days ago and keeping Mom from having *natto* at dinner, but my science project is more important."

Ellen and Little Sister shared a grimace at the memory of the sticky, stinky, slimy mess of soy beans they'd had to choke down. Little Sister obviously hadn't tested her time machine yet if Ellen still remembered their unfortunate dinner.

Little Sister shook her head as if to get rid of the memory

and fiddled with the watch dial again. "Do you want to come with me to meet Galileo?"

Ellen chewed her lip, considering. "I really need to fix my history paper. We should go back to the invention of the tea ceremony."

"What? No, I'm visiting Galileo for my science fair project. We can go see the tea ceremony once I've got the machine out of the prototype stage."

Ellen grabbed at the time machine. "My paper is due next week, I can't wait for the next version. We're going to feudal Japan!"

Little Sister squirmed out of Ellen's reach, clutching the watch against her chest. "My science project is due next week, too! It's my machine, so you'll have to wait."

"I'm older than you," Ellen countered, reaching out again. "Give me that machine!"

"Make your own!"

With a growl like their neighbor's dog, Ellen lunged across the aisle to crash into Little Sister, knocking them both against the shelf of Asian history books. She ignored the books tumbling to the floor around her and grabbed at the yellow watch.

As her finger brushed against the cardboard circle, a sickening jolt tugged somewhere behind her belly button. Colors swirled around her, and the bookshelves melted together into a twirling vortex. Wind roared past Ellen's ears, and the strong scent of copper overwhelmed her. She couldn't feel the library's stiff carpet under her knees anymore.

Lying beside her, Little Sister glared up at Ellen. "What are you doing? Did you even set the time destination?"

"No," Ellen said. "I didn't do anything! How do you work this thing?"

"Let go of it, I'll fix it!"

"No way," Ellen said. "You'll take us to see Galileo. Just tell me how to set it."

As the colors danced around them and the noise rose to the roar of a freight train, Ellen and Little Sister grappled over the yellow wristwatch. Little Sister tugged on the band, and for a moment, Ellen thought she'd lost control of it. With a sharp jerk, she pulled the watch back.

The machine slid out of Little Sister's hands, and the vortex of colors stopped. Heavy heat descended on them, and a sticky-sweet scent rose up from the canopy of green, leafy trees below them.

Ellen screamed. The trees rushed up to meet them, and Ellen braced herself for impact.

Branches and broad leaves whipped at her as she tumbled through them. The snap and crack of breaking branches came like a typhoon. If she made it to the ground with any of her bones unbroken, it would be a miracle.

Finally, the wild descent came to a halt. Her head spun, and it took her a moment to realize she had reached the ground. In fact, she was lying in something cool and wet. She felt it seeping into her hair and school clothes. Ooh, Mom was going to throw a fit.

"Ellen!" Little Sister called from somewhere above her.

Ellen struggled to keep from sinking into the sucking mud and sat up. Her whole body ached, and scratches stung on her arms and legs, but she didn't think any bones were broken. A miracle, after all!

"Ellen, help!" Little Sister cried.

Ellen looked up and found Little Sister dangling from a branch, the back of her school blouse snagged on the end of it. The tree looked odd, with its long, pointy leaves and gray bark, yet Ellen thought she'd seen a picture of something like it before.

Ellen stood and stepped away from the mud puddle. It stank, and the thick heat settling over her made her want to gag. She moved into the huge ferns at the base of Little Sister's tree and hoped the big fronds would scrape some of the mud from her clothes. Instead, the yellow spores hiding on the curled undersides stuck to her skin. Ellen grimaced. She looked like she had a bad, yellow case of the chicken pox.

"Get me down from here," Little Sister said, swinging her legs.

Ellen scowled up at her. "Serves you right. Where are we? *When* are we? This isn't feudal Japan."

"I have no idea! You never even let me look at the time machine. Get me down."

Ellen trudged over to the tree trunk and wrinkled her nose at the long, amber trails of sap oozing all over the rough gray bark. "Ugh, get yourself down. I'm not touching that tree. And if you had just worked with me instead of trying to take us to see Galileo, we wouldn't be in this swamp... jungle... thing."

"You're already all messy," Little Sister pointed out. "You landed in the mud. Look, you got my time machine dirty."

Ellen glanced back at the mud puddle. The yellow wristband flashed out of the muck, the red and blue pipe cleaners looking like they'd been through a particularly clogged pipe.

Ellen tromped back into the sloppy ground, trying not to breathe, and scooped up the watch.

"Maybe I'll just go back home myself," she said, not looking at Little Sister. Risako could always tell when Ellen was lying.

This time was no different. "You can't work the time machine without me. Besides, Mom will ground you for a million years if you leave me in a tree in... whenever this is. Get me down, and I'll figure out when we are."

Ellen sighed. The mud was drying on her skin and clothes, and sweat dripped down her entire body. She was oozing just like that tree, and the unforgiving heat of this place mixed with the stink of the mud puddle made breathing near impossible. She was tired of fighting with Little Sister. They'd both lost their chance at visiting someone in the past. It was time to go home.

"Ellen!" Little Sister screamed.

"I'm coming, I'm coming," Ellen said, turning back.

But Little Sister kept screaming, her eyes bugged out and her arms and legs windmilling like she was trying to backstroke.

The leaves behind Ellen rustled, and she whirled just in time to see a huge, rust-orange creature fly out of the canopy, swooping towards the branch where Little Sister dangled.

Leathery bat-wings sent the humid air swirling, and a long, pointed beak full of tiny teeth opened as the pterodactyl stretched its taloned feet towards Little Sister.

Ellen suddenly remembered the books about prehistoric periods where she'd seen pictures of these strange trees before.

"Risako!" Ellen cried. She stumbled forward, reaching for the tree. She didn't even think of the oozy sap as she wrapped her arms around the trunk.

The pterodactyl screeched, Little Sister shrieked, and Ellen twisted her head up to see the monster flapping up and through the canopy.

Little Sister hung from its claws, her yells growing fainter as the pterodactyl carried her away.

Ellen dropped back down to the muddy ground, tears blurring her vision. She was hot, dirty, her arms and legs stung from a million scrapes, and her sister was about to be a dinosaur's lunch.

Pterodactyls aren't dinosaurs, Little Sister would have said in her know-it-all scientist voice. But Ellen didn't care about the correct classification of the monster that was going to eat her sister.

A huge, prickly insect crawled up Ellen's leg, and she batted it away with a strangled yell. The thing opened its way-too-huge wings and buzzed away with a deep drone. It flew in the same direction the pterodactyl had gone.

Ellen dashed her tears away. Sitting in a stinky mud puddle and crying wasn't going to save Little Sister, and it certainly wasn't going to get her out of the Cretaceous Period and back to the school library.

Brushing what mud she could from herself, she set off through the thick ferns, following the pterodactyl. She tried not to think about how she was following the big insect, too.

What was she going to do? She had no idea where the pterodactyl had gone, and it was certainly flying faster than she was clawing her way through these ferns. Even if she managed to find it again, she had no way of fighting it off of Little Sister.

The time machine's wristband dug into her palm, and she stopped to look at it again. How did it work? It was just an old watch and some pipe cleaners. The hands were unmoving, stuck on 12:00. The cardboard disk hung limply from its pipe cleaner hook, damp from the mud. It had stopped working as soon as it was out of Little Sister's hands. Ellen couldn't fathom how to get it to work again, and she was afraid to try. She didn't actually want to leave Little Sister behind here.

Even though that's what she'd said. It didn't matter that Little Sister had known she was lying. The last thing she'd said to Little Sister was that she wanted to leave her behind in this horrible place, right before she'd been scooped up by a big not-dinosaur.

Tears pricked at her eyes again, but Ellen blinked them away. She'd apologize to Little Sister as soon as she'd rescued her. Then they'd go back home. She tucked the time machine into her skirt pocket.

She struggled against the underbrush until her stomach let out a long, uncomfortable growl. Lunch period had come and gone, and Ellen had skipped it to go to the library.

She found a small patch of open ground and stopped to open her backpack. The bento her mom had packed her sat right on top of her books, and Ellen pulled it out and snapped the plastic lid open. The salty aroma of the seaweed and rice and the faint undertone of the salmon and mayonnaise filling had her stomach growling again. Her favorite. She pulled the first one out and took a big bite.

She finished that one in record time just to make her stomach stop growling. As she picked up the second onigiri, she realized that her stomach wasn't the only thing growling nearby.

Something lurked in the clump of ferns to Ellen's left. Something that sounded big and hungry.

Ellen held herself still despite every instinct screaming at her to bolt. Weren't dinosaurs dependent on sight to hunt? She remembered that from somewhere. Then again, she'd never really kept up with dinosaur research.

The fronds rustled, and a snout like a curved parrot's beak poked out. The scaly nostrils flared, and a whuffling sound filled the tiny clearing.

Ellen clutched her plastic bento box in trembling hands as a big triceratops stepped out of the ferns. Its frill was as big as the chalkboard in Ms. Haley's classroom, and just as green. The three horns curved upwards to end in sharp points. The dinosaur walked right for Ellen.

Ellen squeezed her eyes shut. *Triceratops ate plants*, she chanted to herself. *It doesn't want to eat me.*

Still, the bento box rattled in her hands when the triceratops stopped right in front of her. A musty smell wafted off its scaly hide, and it reminded Ellen of old books.

The triceratops sniffed at the bento box with deep breaths that dragged at Ellen's school clothes and smelled like it really needed to brush its teeth. Then it butted at her with its beak.

Ellen screamed and fell over, but she managed to keep ahold of her bento box. The triceratops took a single step to follow her, and she found herself looking up at its neck and chin.

Maybe the triceratops didn't want to eat her, but that wouldn't stop it from stepping on her!

Luckily, the dinosaur backed up and stuck its beak right into Ellen's face. It nudged at her hands and the bento box.

"What, do you want a snack?" Ellen asked. "You want my onigiri?" Maybe triceratopses liked seaweed and rice and salmon.

An idea formed in Ellen's head. The triceratops didn't have any trouble barreling through the underbrush, unlike her. And she had something he obviously wanted to eat.

A quick scan of the area showed Ellen a supply of branches littering the ground, as well as vines crawling up the wide trunks of the prehistoric trees.

The triceratops nudged at her again, reminding her that he wanted his treat. Ellen fumbled at the lid of her bento while she figured out the rest of her plan. This certainly wasn't the first time she'd shared Japanese food with a strange companion in order to save her own life.

She dug one of the two remaining onigiri out of the bento box and tossed it a little ways away from her. It landed in the dirt with a soft thump.

The triceratops stepped over to it, crushing a fern on the way, and lowered his head to eat.

With her new friend distracted, Ellen rushed to get a sturdy branch, and then she moved to the nearest tree trunk. She wrapped her fingers around a vine and tugged on it. It was just like playing tug-of-war in gym class, right down to the burn of the rope as it slid against her hands, but more was riding on her winning this match than a grade in gym.

Finally, Ellen freed the vine from the tree. While the triceratops finished off his snack, Ellen wrestled the vine, branch, and bento box with the remaining onigiri into a lure.

Her lure finished, Ellen clambered onto the triceratops's back before he could stand back up. She was surprised at how leathery the dinosaur's skin was. She'd thought they had scales like the pet lizards in her science classroom did.

The triceratops stood with a lurch, and Ellen nearly dropped her branch lure. The huge frill rotated away as her new friend tried to look over his shoulder at her. Ellen regained her balance and giggled at the few grains of white rice stuck to the triceratops's beak.

"Okay, 'Tops. You want this other onigiri? You gotta help me rescue Little Sister first."

Ellen slid forward and dangled her bento lure in front of 'Tops's face. Just as she'd hoped, the dangling box and the remaining onigiri drew his attention immediately. Ellen swung the branch in the direction of the pterodactyl's flight.

'Tops bulldozed through the underbrush, while Ellen held onto his frill with one hand and directed him with the lure in the other. She kept her eyes on the canopy of leaves ahead of them, hoping to get some hint of where the pterodactyl had taken Little Sister.

After a while, Ellen pulled the lure up, and 'Tops came to a stop. There'd been no sign of Little Sister or the pterodactyl, and Ellen was afraid they'd lost the trail long ago.

What was she thinking, trying to use a land-bound dinosaur to track a flying kidnapper? And now she was sitting here, hot and stinky, and sleepy, with her skirt pocket vibrating and her only companion a hungry triceratops.

Ellen snapped awake. Her skirt pocket was vibrating! She dug into it and pulled the time machine out. The pipe cleaners were twitching, the cardboard circle was swaying, and the hands of the watch were pointing to Ellen's right. When she twisted that way, the hands swung like a compass needle.

Ellen peered through the dense foliage over that way and thought she could make out a craggy rock face a ways out.

'Tops set off as soon as she dropped the lure before his beak again, and they covered the distance in the time it took Ellen to question her trust of a broken wristwatch. Then again, Little Sister's devices did seem to work best when she was around them.

As they neared the tree line, Ellen spotted a cave high up on the cliff face. A pterodactyl sat there, spreading its giant bat-wings.

A splash of blue and white the exact shades of their school uniforms waved like a flag as the pterodactyl herded Little Sister into its nest.

A surge of victory rushed through Ellen, and she urged 'Tops on faster.

They were just about to break out of the trees when 'Tops came to a shuddering halt. He refused to budge another step, no matter how much Ellen waved the bento box.

"Fine, you lazy bum," she grumbled, sliding off his back. "You couldn't climb those cliffs, anyway. At least I got full marks on the climbing wall in gym."

Ellen set off into the open area, dry dirt and rocks crunching under her school shoes. The area was silent, but at least the air tasted fresh out here. Ellen took a deep, appreciative breath.

Now that she looked at the cliff face from the ground

instead of perched on 'Tops's back, it looked really high. Climbing up there would take hours, and while the open space let a breeze ruffle her hair, the hot sun still beat down relentlessly. She might pass out before she got halfway up!

Unless she got a ride up there.

"Hey, ptero-brain!" Ellen shouted, cupping her hands around her mouth. "My sister's not a big enough snack for you. Come get me, too!"

High above her, the pterodactyl poked its long beak out of its cave.

Ellen waved her arms and shouted some more, but the pterodactyl didn't come any closer.

Exhausted, Ellen slumped forward and panted. Stupid pterodactyl. No wonder they were extinct.

Maybe she could still find a use for 'Tops. There had to be a path she could ride him up. She turned around to walk back to the trees.

Something towered between Ellen and the trees, its mouth open to display its sharp teeth and its cruel talons tearing up the dirt. Its head was tilted so one cantaloupe-sized, yellow eye peered down at her. The crimson feathers along its head, back, and even on its disproportionately tiny arms, didn't look quite the way Ellen remembered from the drawings in her school books, but she still knew the T. rex on sight.

Ellen couldn't help herself. She screamed and dropped her bento box lure as she tore off towards the cliffs at her top speed.

Her feet slapped against the hard ground, sending puffs of dust flying, and her chest heaved as she dragged breath after breath into her lungs.

Behind her, the T. rex followed, its footsteps shaking the earth. It let out a screech that filled Ellen's mind with images of birds of prey swooping in on her. Its hot breath brushed the back of her neck.

Ellen put on another burst of speed and flung herself into the rocks at the cliff bottom. She ducked under a rocky ledge when she felt the snap of massive jaws closing behind her ear.

Pressed against the cliff wall and shaking with fear, Ellen watched the T. rex shuffling around, trying to poke its snout under the ledge.

Finally, the T. rex roared loud enough to rattle every rock in the area and stomped a few paces away to wait for Ellen to come back out.

Ellen scanned her tiny sanctuary for anything she could use. All she found were rocks and more dirt. At least it was cool and dry here in the shade. She'd catch her breath for a moment and figure something out.

The time machine buzzed in her skirt pocket again. She pulled it out to see the hands spinning rapidly. Did that mean Little Sister was directly above her now? Ellen couldn't get any closer without going where the T. rex could catch her.

Ellen scowled and sat down. It would be nice if Little Sister would help out some. Couldn't she find a way to climb down here on her own? Surely she'd seen Ellen come out of the jungle.

A wave of anger washed over her, even though she knew it wasn't fair of her. This was all Little Sister's fault! Ellen wished she could tackle her into the cliff wall like she did at the bookshelves back in the library. Falling rocks would hurt more than falling books, but...

Ellen jerked to her feet. She *could* bring Little Sister down to her! She'd just have to be quick. Very quick.

Ellen stepped out from her little rock ledge and waved her arms at the T. rex.

"Come and eat me, you overgrown chicken!" Ellen shouted.

The T. rex came towards her with thundering steps and gaping jaws. The only thing faster than the dinosaur was its nasty meat-breath.

Ellen forced herself to stay where she was until the T. rex was close enough to bite her in two. As its toothy maw descended like a screaming missile, she scrambled back to her rock ledge and cowered with her arms over her head.

The impact of the massive T. rex into the cliff face sent tremors through the rocks and Ellen. Cracks appeared in the wall, but it wasn't quite enough yet. Ellen saw the dinosaur back up, shaking its head. It turned to walk away.

"No!" Ellen cried. She grabbed up a rock and hurled it after the retreating T. rex.

It howled and swung back around, its yellow eyes rolling in fury. Crimson feathers flew as it charged forward again.

A loud crack reverberated at the second impact, and Ellen ran to avoid the rockslide as the cliff face came crashing down.

"Little Sister!" Ellen yelled once the echoes faded.

Someone coughed in the rubble. Ellen rushed to dig her out, tossing rocks haphazardly until she uncovered Little Sister. A bruise was forming on her cheek, but she didn't look any worse for her tumble from the pterodactyl's cave.

"Wow, what a ride!" Little Sister said. "Nice thinking."

"Take the time machine and get us out of here," Ellen said. She shoved the time machine into Little Sister's hands, and Little Sister tweaked the pipe cleaners and spun the watch dial.

The rocks to their left flew upwards as the T. rex clawed out of them with an earth-shattering roar. It wriggled towards them, moving like it hadn't just been crushed in a rockslide.

Ellen screamed again, and she and Little Sister grabbed each other. They wouldn't be able to move away in time.

A screech pierced out of the sky, and the pterodactyl shot down into the rubble, flapping its wings and jabbing its beak at the T. rex. It screeched again in challenge, then whipped around to face the girls, talons grasping.

Ellen punched at the talon approaching Little Sister. This stupid not-a-dinosaur wouldn't take her sister again.

The pterodactyl rolled around her punch and reached for Ellen instead.

The claws closed around Ellen's shoulders and she was pulled out of the rocks. Little Sister's hand slipped away.

"Take the time machine back home, Risako," Ellen yelled. "Save yourself!"

At least Mom couldn't ground her for a million years if she became ptero-lunch.

The world dropped away below Ellen in a reverse of their arrival in this time, and she swallowed against the urge to scream again. She squeezed her eyes shut.

Her arm jerked hard, and she opened her eyes to find Little Sister dangling from her hand. She'd jumped up at the last moment!

"We're both going home right now," Little Sister called up to her.

"What if we bring the pterodactyl back?" Ellen asked. Just imagine *that* in the library!

"We don't have a choice now. Hold on."

Little Sister fiddled with the time machine and clicked the dial back into place. Something yanked inside Ellen's stomach, and the swirling vortex of colors replaced the blue of the sky. The scent of copper returned, and Ellen no longer saw the ground miles below her. The pterodactyl's grip on her shoulders faded.

The vortex disappeared, and Ellen and Little Sister fell to the floral-patterned library carpet. Something crashed to the floor beside them, and a flat wing blocked the dim light from the ceiling.

"We made it!" Little Sister said, sitting up. Ellen sat up, too, shoving the big papier-mâché model of a pterodactyl off herself. They must have knocked it down upon their arrival.

"What on Earth is going on back here?" a woman cried. The librarian appeared from the bookshelves, her eyes squinty with anger and her fingers twitching for her detention pad like a cowboy at a shootout.

"Sorry, ma'am," Ellen mumbled, grabbing Little Sister's hand and dragging her into the hallway.

The bell rang to signal the end of lunch period. Students poured out of the cafeteria, groaning about the return to class.

Ellen looked at herself and Little Sister. They weren't as dirty as she'd thought, though they were both streaked with dust and small scratches that could be explained away as paper cuts.

"I'm sorry about ruining your prototype test," Ellen said. "And for the things I said back there."

Little Sister shook her head. "It was a pretty good test, anyway. I'll just have to do my science project research the old-fashioned way."

"Yeah, I guess so," Ellen said, thinking of her own history paper.

Little Sister waved goodbye and headed down the first-grader hallway.

Ellen sighed. She needed to head to class, too. Shrugging her backpack onto a shoulder, she glanced back at the library.

For some reason, the heavy doors didn't look so intimidating anymore. What were silly library ghosts compared to facing down a T. rex?

Although Mom might ground her for a million years for leaving her bento box in the Cretaceous Period!

THREE

The Underwater Conundrum

Ellen Sugimori had long since come to terms with the fact that her Japanese ancestry required her to attend Japanese school on weekends, even now in the summer, but when she glanced out the window to see a group of her American friends walking by and enjoying their freedom while she sat trapped in the stuffy community center classroom, tingles of jealousy zinged through her whole body.

Despite that, Ellen kept staring out the window beside her. The community center park grounds spread out invitingly just beyond the thick pane, green grass rolling like waves. In the distance, the Detroit skyline rose like an ocean-side cliff. Full-leafed trees rustled in the wind and danced like sea spray.

The three kids she recognized from school strolled along, laughing in the sunlight and carrying backpacks bristling with pool toys. The boys were already wearing their swim trunks, and the girl wore a t-shirt over her own suit. Looking at them,

Ellen could almost taste the yellowy-green of summer. She took a deep breath without thinking, and choked on stale classroom air.

Ellen recovered with a few gulps and turned back to the front. It was almost three o'clock, and Honda-sensei reached for the stack of homework packets on his desk. Impatient for her own moment of freedom, Ellen scooped her notebooks into her backpack. Then she arched her back until her spine popped. The community center chairs made the desk seats at school seem like fluffy beanbag chairs in comparison.

What she'd really like to do after a long day at Japanese school was to go home, open the window in her bedroom, and read the next book in her current manga series. But finding out what happened next in the saga of *Neko-hime*, who turned into a cat whenever she was embarrassed, and who was currently trapped in a world of dog shape-shifters, would have to wait until after dinner at least. Ellen still had to meet Little Sister at the pool for their daily swimming lesson.

Or rather, Ellen thought with a grumpy rumble in her throat, her daily "attempt to get Risako to even put her feet in the water" lessons. If Ellen couldn't get Little Sister to demonstrate at least a respectable dog-paddle by the beginning of August, her parents wouldn't take them to the beach at all. Time was running short now that summer was half gone. No matter what Ellen tried, shouting, threatening, pleading, it had no effect. It left Ellen with only one conclusion.

Little Sister was trying to sabotage her beach trip dreams.

"Sugimori-*chan, daijoubu?* Are you all right?"

Ellen jumped at Honda-sensei's voice. Pain in her jaw told her she'd been clenching her teeth again, and she relaxed and took the homework packet he held.

"*Hai, sensei. Daijoubu desu.* I just have to meet my sister at the pool." And convince her to get her butt in the water before it's too late.

Slinging her backpack over her shoulder, Ellen bowed to Honda-sensei in thanks for the lesson, and then headed out of the classroom. She promised herself right now she would not fail at the swimming lesson today. She would get to the beach at the end of summer, no matter if she had to toss Little Sister in the pool herself.

To get to the pool, Ellen had to walk through the community center hallway where pictures of "important contributors" stared boringly from the walls, then go outside and cross the picnic area, before finally arriving at the pool entrance. She showed her membership card to the high schooler manning the gate, then pushed through the one-way rotating bars. She tried to tuck her backpack under her arm, but like always, it caught on the bars behind her, and she had to jerk it loose. She made a quick stop in the locker room to change into her swimsuit.

The harsh scent of chlorine and over-sweet sunscreen hit her in the nose like a combo punch. Ellen supposed over-bleaching was better than having to swim in a dirty pool, but it always took her a few breaths to adjust to it. Blinking as her eyes streamed, she scanned the area for Little Sister.

When she found her, sitting on a deck chair beyond the kiddie pool, Ellen groaned. Little Sister had one of her cardboard boxes beside her. Ellen recognized some of Little Sister's "science projects" sticking out of it.

Ellen stomped around the kiddie pool, skirting a boy comforting his toddler brother who was howling that he'd dropped something in the deep end, and came up behind Little Sister.

"Risako," Ellen said, mimicking how *Kaa-san,* their mother, snapped the name out when they were in trouble. It didn't seem to have the terrifying effect she was going for, since Little Sister just blinked up at her with an expression of vague interest.

"Oh, you're here. Finally."

Little Sister reached for her box, and Ellen grabbed her hand. "No, not today. None of your adventures until you learn to swim, okay?"

Little Sister jerked her hand out of Ellen's grip. "But I've been working on a design for a diving suit. It's ready for testing, and I need your help."

She rummaged in the box, shoving aside a pair of cardboard tube thrusters from her rocket ship and a tangle of pipe cleaners. When she emerged, she had one of their dad's old Tigers t-shirts in each hand.

Heavily modified, of course. Ellen groaned again.

Little Sister spread one out so Ellen could see the big plastic food container she'd duct-taped to the back and the tangle of rubber tubing snaking between it and an old painter's mask.

"These should let us dive and explore underwater without having to worry about drowning. See, the air comes from the tank, and then we can breathe it. Here, put this one on."

Little Sister thrust the shirt at Ellen.

"I'm not wearing that! Come on, put that away and let's get to the swimming lesson. You're embarrassing me."

Little Sister hopped off the deck chair and tugged the other modified shirt over her own head. The thing fell past her knees. When she put the mask over her face, it made her look like some kind of bug-creature. She dug in her cardboard box again, and came away with a nylon bag tied to her wrist. It clanked with various science tools inside.

Ellen slapped her hand against her forehead. "Risako!"

Little Sister held the other shirt to her again. "I'm not getting in the water unless you help me test the suit out. I don't like swimming, but there's important stuff I need to study down there, and this suit should help me do it. I promise I'll let you give me lessons, but you have to help me with this first."

Ellen considered the offer. She'd been trying for over a month to get Little Sister to swim. But a quick glance around the pool showed a number of people, including those kids from school over in the deep end. How quickly would word spread among her friends if she wore this ridiculous shirt? What if they took pictures?

Ellen closed her eyes. Her mind filled with thoughts of the ocean, and salt brine replaced the chlorine burn. Gritty sand scuffed beneath her bare feet instead of smooth poolside concrete. The shrieks of the kids turned into the cries of seagulls. She wanted to go to the beach so much it hurt.

The illusion shattered when she opened her eyes, but Little Sister still stood before her, the shirt in her fist.

Ellen snatched it away. "Fine, I'll play."

"Great!"

Ellen slipped the huge shirt over her head. Her arms got tangled in the labyrinth of cotton, and while her head searched for the collar, something splashed into the pool right beside her. She found the hole, only to discover that Little Sister had vanished.

In the pool, bubbles blorped above a dark shape near the bottom.

"Risako!" Ellen shouted. Her heart thumped so hard the plastic container taped to her back bounced against her spine. Little Sister had jumped in without so much as a single swimming lesson!

Ellen was so angry she could taste it, like three-day-old *natto* mixed with rubbery bits of squid and a big dollop of *wasabi*.

Kaa-san would ground her for life if she let Little Sister drown. Grabbing the stupid painter's mask, Ellen sucked in a lungful of air and jumped in after her.

Despite expecting the sting of chlorine, she kept her eyes open as the water closed over her head. But instead of the blue and white tiles of the pool walls and floor, a rocky reef full of colorful polyps and waving tendrils of seaweed greeted her.

Ellen somehow managed to keep from gasping in surprise. She brought the painter's mask up to her face and took a tentative breath. Little Sister's diving suit worked, somehow. Ellen never asked about the science behind these projects.

Okay, so she wasn't going to drown, which probably meant Little Sister was safe, too, despite how she'd just let herself sink like a rock. Still, Ellen wasn't going to let the troublesome scientist out of her sight in the middle of the ocean. Angling herself downwards, she fluttered her legs. Bubbles escaped from her mask and drifted upward.

The ocean! The saltwater washed around her, a slight pull this way and that as the water moved with the waves overhead. Fish flashed by, shafts of sunlight playing on their bright scales. In the murky distance, dark shapes drifted, lurking. The reef extended far out to either side of her, but in front of her the sea floor descended until it dropped away into the open ocean over a deep, dark trench.

Ellen couldn't help grinning. If she'd realized helping Little Sister with her latest experiment would get her to the ocean without her parents' half-promise, she'd have put the stupid shirt on without a fight.

She pushed herself all the way down to where Little Sister sat surrounded by pink and orange anemones, pawing through her science bag. Little Sister looked up as she approached. Bubbles rose from her mask, and Ellen wondered if she was trying to talk. She couldn't hear anything but the burbling of the ocean.

Ellen shook her head and pointed to her ears, then motioned to Little Sister to get up. She had to teach Little Sister how to swim before any science could be done.

Little Sister struggled to a half-standing, half-drifting position. The oversized t-shirt billowed around her like a watermaid's gown. Ellen took her hand and pulled her a little away from the reef so they'd have room to swim. Little Sister's grip tightened, but Ellen was a good swimmer, and she moved them along without a hitch.

Luckily, Little Sister sucked up knowledge like a sponge when she actually tried. It wasn't long before Little Sister was able to move on her own and keep herself from drifting off in the undertow.

During their lesson, schools of fish swam all around them and the reef. Once Ellen was certain Little Sister had the basics down, they took a break and floated by a rocky outcropping to watch the different sea creatures flitting by. A forest of seaweed danced just beyond the rocks of the reef. Every color had a fish representing it in the warm water, and little red and green crabs scuttled to and fro in the sandy rocks. Ellen gasped as what she thought was a chunk of rock suddenly flushed red and became an octopus.

Little Sister tugged at Ellen's arm. Ellen turned to see Little Sister's eyes crinkled, though her bubbling mask concealed her smile.

Before Ellen could return the smile, a huge school full of fish the size of footballs burst out from the seaweed forest behind Little Sister. The fish angled directly for the two of them.

Ellen shrieked and grabbed the back of Little Sister's diving suit to yank her out of the way. They had nowhere to go but towards the reef, and Ellen scraped her elbow a little as they squeezed close to let the fish rush past them. She hissed at the sting, and bubbles rose from her mask in a thin stream.

When the last of the school finally wriggled past, Ellen let go of Little Sister and touched her elbow. Her fingers came away red, and a tiny wisp of blood threaded through the water. She grimaced. Blood didn't make her feel sick, but she hated dealing with it. The salt water made the cut sting more, too.

Little Sister tugged on her diving suit, but Ellen swatted her away. Cleaning up a cut on her elbow was awkward enough without her sister pointing out every little thing that caught her attention. Pulling the bottom of the huge t-shirt up, she blotted it over the cut. Little Sister had already mutilated the shirt, so Ellen didn't think *Tou-san* would mind her getting a little blood on it.

Little Sister gave a sharper pull, and the fabric slipped out of Ellen's hand. Growling, Ellen rounded on Little Sister.

A wash of frigid cold swept over her when she saw the shark Little Sister pointed at. The creature snaked through the water, tail swishing back and forth as it drew closer, but its snout and beady black eyes remained fixed on them. Only a few tail swishes remained between it and them.

Another wisp of red from her elbow curled in front of her eyes.

Ellen screamed and clawed at Little Sister. Little Sister didn't move, staring wide-eyed at the shark like she'd forgotten how to blink.

The shark opened its jaws. Ellen counted at least three rows of glimmering teeth before she realized the counting was a stupid waste of time.

"Come on!" she shouted.

Lugging Little Sister with her, Ellen kicked away from the

seaweed forest. She couldn't hide in a place where she couldn't see the shark, but it could still smell her and sneak up on her.

Little Sister still hadn't remembered how to move at all. Her weight pulled on Ellen's arm, dragging them downwards. Ellen spared a glance over her shoulder as she struggled to keep moving and search for a place to hide.

The shark's nose twitched an arm's length away from Little Sister.

Ellen wouldn't let Little Sister become shark chum. With a grunt, she twisted herself so she swam between Little Sister and the shark. She used both hands to hold Little Sister steady, then kicked as hard as she could towards the reef, and hopefully shelter.

Little Sister pointed out into the open ocean. More pointy shark shapes emerged from the murk over the blackness of the deep water, three, four, five of them all converging on them.

All of them looked hungry.

Along the length of the reef, fish darted into tiny hide-holes. Ellen watched them, hoping for one of them to lead her to a hole big enough for the two of them.

There! A big purple fish ducked into a round opening in the reef under a big, flat piece of coral. Ellen fluttered her legs hard, steering Little Sister that way. Little Sister seemed to pick up on the idea, and windmilled her arms.

Little Sister grabbed at the rocky edges of the hole, and Ellen shoved at her back to get her inside. She didn't dare glance over her shoulder, but as she got her own hands on the hole, a sudden impact sent her jolting forward.

On her next breath, water poured into her mask.

The first shark had rammed into her air tank!

Holding her breath, Ellen kicked the shark in the snout. Its rough skin scraped at her heel, but the creature turned away. It shook its snout, then turned back to Ellen. Its jaws opened wide.

Ellen pulled herself into the hole before the shark could chomp on her. She wanted very much to sit there in the safety of the cave and catch her breath, but water still burbled through her mask.

She could either drown in here or start a feeding frenzy out there.

Lots of little holes in the reef let enough light into this cave to keep it from being pitch black, but the darkness still pressed Ellen into panic mode. Her lungs ached with urgency. And where had Little Sister gone?

As if on cue, Little Sister appeared from above her. She grabbed Ellen's shoulder and pointed upwards. Above them, faint light rippled on the surface of the water.

Ellen flailed towards it. Her lungs burned now, desperate for air.

When she broke the surface, she tore the mask away and gasped. The sound echoed off the water and the rocks of the cave.

Once she had gulped enough air that she could think straight, Ellen looked around their refuge.

The cave yawned wider than she had assumed from the size of the hole. The ceiling stood high above her head, giving her plenty of air. A briny, fishy smell coated the rocks, even stronger than the fish market section of the Asian grocery story *Kaa-san* took them to every week. At the top of the ceiling, a cluster of small holes let pure sunlight filter into the cave. The reef must poke above the water here.

But fat drops of water dripped from the walls higher up. That meant this pocket of air might not always be here, and the holes up there didn't look big enough for Ellen to wriggle through.

Beside her, Little Sister splashed and flailed.

Ellen sighed. "You have to tread water like this. Move your arms and legs at the same time."

Once Little Sister got herself bobbing steadily, she pulled her mask off. "Maybe those sharks are gone now?"

"I don't know," Ellen said. "Even if they are, how am I going to get out of here? My tank's broken."

She held up her own mask for Little Sister to look at. She realized now that the whole rubber hose was missing.

Little Sister paddled around to poke at the tank on Ellen's back. "It's cracked, too. If we had the hose still, I could just reattach it, but this crack is really big."

Ellen swallowed against a bitter lump in her throat. "I can't hold my breath long enough to get back down to that hole and also up to the surface again."

"Hey, you might not have to hold it that long. Those sharks looked really hungry."

"That's not funny," Ellen said.

"Maybe there's another way out," Little Sister said and gave a funny wiggle. She pulled a waterproof flashlight from her science bag, and light flooded the cave. Blinded, Ellen threw a hand over her eyes and blinked the spots away.

Little Sister swung the beam around in an erratic pattern as she kept treading water. Ellen strained her eyes, but with the shadows dancing so much, she couldn't tell where a hole might be. As far as she could make out, they were encased in rocks and water, except for holes too small to get through.

Then the light glimmered off something that wasn't rock or water. It wasn't a fish, either, though it kind of resembled one with glass windows like bulbous eyes at the front and a propeller system of streamlined fins on the sides and back. The metal sheeting on the outside flashed like fish scales when the light passed over it. At the top, a closed hatch took the place of a dorsal fin.

"A submarine!" Little Sister said. "We can use that to get out."

"It's way bigger than the hole we came in through, though," Ellen said.

"Then there must be a bigger hole somewhere else."

Ellen followed as Little Sister splashed over to the abandoned submarine. It rested on a shelf of rock like a toy waiting to be played with again. It must have gotten there when the water filled the cave all the way to the top, but now it was stuck.

"Does it even work?" she asked.

Little Sister had already clambered onto the shelf beside it and had her science bag open. "It just needs a few modifications." She peered through one of the windows and grimaced back at Ellen. "It's got an air tank in it, but the space is only big enough for one person."

Ellen grasped the edge of the shelf and chewed on her lip. "That means... I'll have to go in it. Your diving suit's air tank still works."

Little Sister nodded and opened the hatch to poke her head in. "I can definitely get this working. I've got plenty of pipe cleaners, but I think I'm going to have to sacrifice the flashlight to make the power cell."

Then she disappeared back into the submarine, and the clanks and hisses of science being done echoed out through the hatch.

Ellen treaded water and held onto the rocky shelf. The water had risen since she'd come over here, and it lapped at her fingers and washed over the edge of the shelf. She tilted her head back and looked at the ceiling. The panic was creeping up on her again.

A mechanical rumble vibrated from the submarine, and the

motor hummed. Little Sister popped out of the hatch with a wide grin.

"It works! Help me push it into the water."

"It's practically already back in the water," Ellen grumbled, but she pulled herself onto the shelf anyway. Together at the back of the sub, she and Little Sister braced themselves against the barnacle-studded cave wall and shoved. The sub slid off the shelf and bobbed like a toy boat, slowly drifting away from them.

"Okay, you get in, find a way out, and scare the sharks off," Little Sister said. "Then I can swim out and you can drive the sub up to the surface."

Ellen wanted to tell Little Sister not to order her around, but it was a good plan, so she clamped her mouth shut and jumped for the submarine. Gripping the slippery outside took effort, but somehow she got herself flipped inside it and the hatch shut before any water could slop over the opening.

She found herself kneeling in a cramped space. With the hatch closed, she had to hunch her shoulders to keep from hitting her head, and she didn't have room to stretch her legs. In the back, Little Sister had left a tangled mess of pipe cleaners and duct tape attached to a jittering motor. The waterproof flashlight shone from inside the tangle, its beam angled so it only halfway shone out the front window. The dashboard at the front end had more buttons than *Tou-san's* car, but at least an obvious joystick in the middle presented an easy method of steering. A second, smaller joystick sat on the right side by the window.

Awkward in the small space, Ellen scooted up to the front. She could make out the shape of Little Sister dog-paddling outside. Little Sister waved at her, then pointed downward.

Ellen took a deep breath and took the big joystick in hand. The idea of driving this thing without Little Sister's help freaked her out. What if something went wrong that she couldn't fix?

But with her limited air supply and those sharks patrolling right outside the little entrance, she didn't have any choice. Palms dripping with seawater and sweat, she nosed the submarine into a dive.

The flashlight's thin beam rippled through the front window as Ellen descended. It played over the walls of the cave, illuminating colorful coral and sending fish darting out of the way. Ellen focused on finding the way out.

She descended almost to the sandy bottom, past the hole they'd come in through. A quick glance out the side window showed the menacing silhouettes of sharks cruising out there. Ellen gulped and scanned the rocks below.

In a shadowy nook, a tumble of rocks and gently waving anemone tendrils hid the opening she needed. Ellen pressed forward with more speed, and the rumble of the motor vibrated through the sub as it churned into the tunnel. Almost immediately, the tunnel curved downwards in a crooked left-hand helix. With the flashlight pointed in the top right corner of her window, Ellen had to drive practically blind through the winding course.

The tunnel kept going, downward and downward, and the farther down she went, the more darkness crept into the space. Her ears popped with the pressure difference, and she wiggled her jaw around until they opened again. Strange sounds, like ringing cracks and wavering moans, reverberated through the tunnel, layering on top of the submarine's *chuk-chuk-chuk*. Whether the sounds came from behind her or ahead, she had no way of telling.

Finally, the path evened out, and the rocky passage widened. Beyond the beam of her flashlight, the water pressed in with utter blackness. The sounds continued, eerie and shivery. The cold of the water this deep penetrated the hull of her sub, and Ellen shuddered in her wet t-shirt.

She'd apparently emerged in the deep trench beyond the reef. The fact that her light wasn't positioned well didn't help calm her nerves any, but she didn't dare adjust it. Little Sister's contraptions worked in their own way, and Ellen had no intention of messing up the rig. She would have to make do with the tiny sliver of useful light as she found her way out of the terrifying trench.

She should be able to drive the sub straight up, right?

Up proved a little more difficult than down. The joystick didn't work the way she expected it would. A lever on the left of the dashboard rested in the down position, and Ellen flipped it with shaking fingers. The motor gave a loud *kerchunk*, and the submarine lurched upwards.

Ellen let out a deep sigh. Her heart pounded against her ribs, and she shivered uncontrollably. When she'd asked to visit the ocean, exploring a scary deep sea trench was not what she'd had in mind. Having to rely on Little Sister's jury-rigged submarine made everything just that much worse. Sure, it was working now, but it rattled and coughed like it was on its last fins. Besides, Little Sister's machines tended to work best when she was nearby. The further away from her they got, the more they malfunctioned.

And who knew what sort of monstrous, man-eating sea creatures Ellen might find down here?

As soon as the question entered her mind, a clank and a loud screech brought the submarine to a grinding halt. Ellen screamed and slapped her hands over her mouth. She'd been caught! Something must have her in its toothy jaws, and now she was done for.

The screech continued until Ellen winced at its piercing shrillness. That wasn't the sound of teeth. At least, she didn't think it was. It sounded more like rock on metal. The sub must have run into a rock ledge, and though the motor tried its hardest, it couldn't propel the sub through solid rock.

Catching her breath, Ellen took the joystick again. She threw the lever on the side back to the down position and eased the sub around, sweeping the sliver of light in an arc so she might find out where she could go from here.

As she spun, the smooth rock of the trench wall that had been behind her came into view. That was good. If she kept turning another half-circle, she should be able to drive forward a bit, and then go up once she cleared the ledge that had her pinned.

A bright glimmer flashed through the window. Ellen tugged at the joystick to stop her spin and pressed herself against the glass to peer out at the source.

Resting in a crevice packed with clean-picked fish bones, a golden statuette reflected Ellen's tiny light back at her.

"Pretty," she whispered. Her breath fogged the glass, and she wiped at it with her palm.

She was certainly owed a reward for braving this dark trench. She'd been thinking of making Little Sister buy her an ice cream later, but a golden statuette would make a way cooler trophy.

Submarines were vehicles of science. They needed some way of collecting samples from the environment, right?

Ellen ran her hands over the dashboard. A switch on the right by the smaller joystick looked promising. She flipped the switch, and a whine of rusty metal preceded the appearance of a long, thin arm extending just below the window. Using the little joystick, Ellen directed the arm towards the statuette. A set of pincers at the end fastened around it, and Ellen reeled it back in.

A series of clunks sounded in the floor, and suddenly the statuette appeared in a clear pipe to Ellen's right.

Feeling much better, Ellen grinned and turned the submarine to the right.

Halfway through the turn, the flashlight beam fell on a pair of giant red tentacles whipping towards her from out of the darkness. They slapped into the submarine with a sucking squelch.

One humongous suction cup covered most of the front window. It left just enough room for the sliver of light to illuminate the body of the giant squid.

All the blood in Ellen's body drained down to her feet. The submarine gave a lurch, and Ellen realized the giant squid was dragging her back down into the depths.

Among the tangle of tentacles, its sharp beak clacked ravenously. As it tugged on the sub, the light shone on a whole hoard of lost treasures, all strewn about the nest of this slavering sea beast.

Ellen threw herself against the dashboard and slammed the lever back into the up position. No way was she letting some giant squid add her to its collection.

The submarine shuddered, and the motor chugged. Metal shrieked as the squid tightened its tentacles.

With a mechanical cough, the motor sputtered. The flashlight flickered.

Ellen wriggled herself around in the tight space until her feet pointed towards the motor, then she gave it a good, solid kick.

"Come on," she yelled.

The motor roared back to life, and the flashlight kicked back on. Ellen felt the sub straining against the squid's hold, jerking upwards like a dog on a leash.

Still, the squid held fast.

Gritting her teeth, Ellen grabbed the smaller joystick. She didn't have time for careful precision, but she swiped the collection arm at the tentacle on her window and pinched the pincers shut.

A squeal like a baritone pig echoed through the trench, and the suction cup pulled away with a loud pop.

Ellen jammed the big joystick around as the suddenly free motor propelled the submarine upwards. Thank goodness the sub had no rear window, or else the temptation to look over her shoulder would slow her down.

Still, she could tell the squid was chasing after her. One did not pinch a squid's tentacle and expect to get away easy, after all. Ellen drove the sub as fast as it would go, pushing it to the point of rattling.

The water around her grew brighter as she climbed higher. Flashes of movement out the side windows as the squid tried to get its tentacles around her again drove her to keep going, despite the way the submarine shuddered. A high whine rang through the sub, and something hissed behind her.

A bolt popped loose to her right, and a spray of seawater drenched her.

"Oh, no," she moaned. The sub had to make it to the surface, or at least to the swarm of sharks.

But as the rock walls of the deep trench fell away below her and she shot into the open water by the reef, the sub continued to disintegrate around her.

Up above, the distinct shapes of sharks writhed around the reef. From below, the giant squid's tentacles lashed at the windows.

Ellen did the only thing she could think of.

Screaming out a battle cry, she drove the sub into the heart of the mass of sharks. She waved the collection arm around, pinching sharks left and right.

The sharks thrashed into a frenzy of rage, but when they

turned their gaping jaws on Ellen and her submarine, she threw the side lever into the down position.

She dived back into the tangle of tentacles. The sharks followed, but when they slammed their jaws shut, it wasn't metal and 12-year-old girl they chomped.

It was giant squid tentacle.

Angry giant squid tentacle.

Ellen wove the submarine through the confusion of the battle of the sea monsters, holding her breath and hoping with everything she had that the sub would hold together. Water from the leak had already filled the chamber a third of the way, and the motor screamed at her that it couldn't give her any more power.

She broke free of the chaos and scanned the reef. Little Sister floated there, paddling out of the cave while the sharks were distracted. She flashed a smile at Ellen, then made for the surface.

Ellen didn't hesitate to follow. She pressed on the joystick, but the sub had taken all it could take. With a series of pops like gunshots, the whole thing fell to pieces. Ellen had just enough time to suck in a huge lungful of air and snatch her statuette prize from the collection container.

Then she was swimming like she'd never swum before. The saltwater burbled in her ears and stung her eyes, and every muscle in her body burned with exhaustion and the need for oxygen.

When her head broke the surface, she gasped and blinked against the harsh burn of chlorine. She wiped the water from her eyes to find Little Sister sitting on the concrete edge of the pool, her painter's mask dangling against her chest.

"That was brilliant," Little Sister called. "Shark against squid!"

Ellen panted and paddled awkwardly to the side of the pool.

She held on one-handed and pulled her other hand up to look at her prize.

"Hey," said a voice above her. A boy a couple years younger than her stood beside the pool, his hands on his knees. "You got my little brother's action figure."

Ellen blinked. She did indeed hold an action figure. She'd squeezed it so tight its pose-able arms dug into her palm.

"Oh," she said. "Yeah, I uh, just saw it down there."

She reached up and handed it to him.

"Thanks! I can't keep my eyes open underwater. It stings too much, and I didn't bring my goggles today."

"No problem," Ellen said as he trotted off.

Little Sister *hmm*ed as Ellen pulled herself up to sit beside her. "The suits need a little more work. They're okay, but they need to be shark-proof if I'm going to study them any closer."

Ellen blanched. "You want to study the *sharks*?"

"I think they're really cool."

"They tried to eat us!"

"Well, they were hungry. You try to eat stuff when you're hungry, right?"

Ellen kicked at the water. "I guess so. But count me out on getting near the sharks again."

In fact, she'd had enough of being in the ocean to last her a while. Oh, she still intended to cash in on the beach trip. Little Sister knew how to swim now, and since she'd lost the golden statuette, she was owed *something* for this ordeal.

But she'd spend the trip safely on the sand, under an umbrella, and reading the next book in the saga of *Neko-hime*!

Four

The Multiplier Malfunction

Ellen Sugimori trudged up the driveway, the straps of her backpack digging into her shoulders. The weight of her books after a long day of school reminded her that she had a mountain of homework and chores to do tonight before she went straight to bed. No video games, no TV, and definitely no next book of her favorite manga series, *Neko-Hime*, were allowed to her until she could show her parents an A grade on her next math test.

Her steps slowed as she mounted the front porch. She sucked in a deep breath, letting the crisp autumn air cool her for a little longer before she had to go inside. The thought of opening the front door sent Ellen's heart plummeting into her shoes. She knew she'd find Little Sister on the other side, enjoying her freedom as she had every day since Mom and Dad had come back from their conference with Ellen's teacher, their faces creased with disappointment.

It wasn't fair. Little Sister didn't have a lick of trouble with math.

For some reason, everyone seemed to think Ellen ought to have just as easy a time, but it wasn't so. She could stare at an equation until her brain throbbed, but the solution would remain hidden more often than not. Her school offered tutors, but the thought of asking a fellow student for help embarrassed her too much. Better to simply not do her math homework and have everyone think she was lazy than to let her classmates know the truth, or so she used to think.

Off in the distance, the church bells chimed four times. Ellen scowled over her shoulder in their direction. They ought to feel guilty for allowing time to continue flowing, especially when she had none to waste. What with her extra math homework on top of her regular homework, and the extra chores that served as her punishment for not studying as much as she should have, she'd be lucky to make even a tiny dent in her work before dinner. Hiking her backpack higher on her shoulders, Ellen opened the door and went inside.

She'd toed her shoes off and had one house slipper on when Mom stepped into the hall. Mom had her nice silk jacket on and her hair done up in the same tight bun she'd worn to meet with Ellen's teacher last week. The pinched expression on her face matched the one she'd come back with that night, too.

Ellen wanted to shrink until she was invisible, but she made herself look Mom in the eye.

"Hi, Mom." Ellen's voice sounded squeaky and small, and she winced at it.

"Eriko," Mom said, using Ellen's Japanese name. "I'm glad you're back. Dinner is ready for you in the refrigerator. All you have to do is warm it up when you and Risako are ready to eat."

"You're going somewhere?" Ellen asked.

Mom gave her a strained look, her eyes sagging like she was

as tired as Ellen felt. "Tonight is our meeting with Risako's teacher, remember? We need you to keep an eye on her. You're a big girl, you can do it."

As exhausted as Ellen's catch-up work had left her, she had forgotten about Little Sister's upcoming teacher conference. A sick feeling churned in her stomach. Keeping Little Sister out of trouble often turned into a full-time job, one she definitely couldn't handle on top of everything else on her plate tonight. She squeezed her backpack straps where they still bit into her shoulders. "Are...are you sure? I know you and Dad are still mad at me..."

"Your father and I expect you to continue your studies as you've been told, but we also trust that you can watch your sister for the evening. You've done a fine job of it before. Just make sure all of your chores are done by the time we get home."

Easy for her to say. Mom wouldn't be the one struggling to get a grasp on factors and wash the dishes all while Little Sister tinkered with her latest science experiment.

Ellen didn't understand how Risako's various scientific machines worked. All Ellen knew was, somehow, Little Sister's rocket ship built from cardboard had flown them to Mars once, and her scuba gear made from old painter's masks had turned a visit to the local pool into a coral reef expedition. Maybe it was because Risako understood math better than Ellen did.

With no parental authority at home, Ellen would be lucky to keep Little Sister from turning the living room into a large particle collider *and* get her math homework done by the time their parents came back.

Mom moved past where Ellen still hunched in the entryway and put her shoes on. "I'm meeting your father at the school. Have a good night, Eriko. Study hard."

Oh, Mom had no idea how hard tonight was going to be.

Ellen clomped through the kitchen, intending to drop her backpack upstairs in her bedroom and bring only the books she needed to study back down. Then she entered the living room, and had to stop immediately.

Finding herself face-to-face with three Risakos, especially when she'd been hoping for *none*, completely derailed her homework plans.

As if the abundance of Little Sisters wasn't enough, the living room looked like a craft shop had exploded inside it. The mess of cardboard clippings, pipe cleaners, and *glitter*—why glitter? What possible scientific use did glitter have?—had Ellen gasping as though she'd stubbed her toe on a particularly sneaky crack in the sidewalk.

Mom hated glitter, and Ellen could just picture what would happen when Mom came home and saw the sparkly stuff everywhere. Worse, she'd think Ellen had allowed Risako to use it.

"You're home!" said one of the Little Sisters, walking towards Ellen. Her face, hands, and hair sparkled.

Another Risako looked up at Ellen. "Good, I need your help with my multiplier machine. I've run into an unexpected problem."

"What? I called dibs on her help first!" said the third Risako.

Maybe Ellen should just head straight back to the kitchen table and open her math book. Or her history book. Honestly, she had homework in every subject. There was no point in wasting time taking the one book she didn't need upstairs, and she had too much work to do to spare even part of her brainpower trying to figure out what mess Little Sister had made this time.

Ellen turned back to the kitchen. Her backpack had gotten heavier, she would swear.

"Come on, Ellen. You always help me test out my prototype machines," the closest Little Sister said. She tugged on Ellen's backpack, almost making Ellen topple backwards.

"Stop that," Ellen said. "I don't have time to help you today. Sort yourself out this time."

Little Sister—the closest one—didn't let go, but she did stop tugging. "But this machine is for you. Well, the final product will be, anyway. I'm testing it out on myself because my reading teacher assigned us three whole books to read tonight, and I don't have time to do all that and work on the improvements to my rocket ship."

Ellen glanced at the corner of the sofa, where a stack of first-grade chapter books lay in an unsteady stack. As a sixth-grader, Ellen would be able to fly through those flimsy things in an hour or two, tops. Since the first-graders got out an hour earlier than the older kids, Little Sister had already been at home for long enough to have made a decent start.

Ellen scowled at all three Risakos. "So you decided to waste time glitterizing the living room instead of just sitting down and doing the work? Didn't you listen at all when Mom and Dad yelled at me about not doing my math homework?"

"The glitter is an important component in the copying mechanism of my multiplier machine," said the Little Sister who sat cross-legged beside the coffee table. "Its ability to persistently stick to any surface helps define the body area to be copied."

"And math homework is fun," said the third Little Sister. She fiddled with a strange device in her hands. It looked like a shoebox cut down to the size of a music box and painted gray. She had the front panel flipped open to expose a coil of red and blue pipe cleaners and...

"Is that a canister of spray glitter?" Ellen screeched. "Are you crazy?"

All three Little Sisters rolled their eyes. "Gosh, you sound like Mom."

"I do not," Ellen retorted automatically. She shook her head. "Look, I really don't have time for this science stuff today. You...three...have to clean all this glitter up right now, then sort yourselves out and do your reading homework."

She fixed them all with her best glare—an imitation of Mom, to be sure, but she wouldn't admit it aloud—until all three Little Sisters nodded, and then she went into the kitchen.

At the kitchen table, she tried her hardest to block out the crashing and banging coming from the living room. She dragged her heavy math book out and opened it to the chapter she was meant to work on tonight. The chapter head declared the topic of study to be "Factors and Fractions," and Ellen held back a groan of despair. Now that the math sat before her, she understood how Little Sister had been driven to work on something else. Homework was so boring when the next book of *Neko-Hime* sent out its siren call from her bedroom.

Even doing questionable science with Little Sister had more appeal than cramming more numbers into her head. But Ellen shoved all those temptations aside and bent over her worksheet. She knew the consequences of not doing the work, and she had no time to put it off, no matter what.

She applied herself so much that the sounds in the living room faded into dull background noise, which was good. She made out raised voices now and then as the three Little Sisters argued about "original" something or other, but she kept her attention focused on her work. Now if only she could actually make some progress, she'd have something to be proud of herself about. But the numbers and symbols all jumbled up on her, until her head throbbed and her fingers cramped around her pencil as she erased yet another wrong answer.

Ellen pressed a hand against her aching forehead. She'd never get this stuff down. Math just wasn't her subject.

Maybe she should take a break and work on her history homework. They were studying Chinese history, and Ellen found the similarities and differences between China and Japan fascinating. Yes, that's what she'd do, let her brain rest a little with something she understood already.

She twisted in her chair to reach for her backpack and the history book.

Six Little Sisters stood in the doorway, all wearing expressions of frustration and about a pound of glitter each.

"I really need your help, Ellen," said the left-most Little Sister.

Ellen dropped her head onto her open math book. She should have known better than to hope this problem would go away if she ignored it. Now it had quite literally multiplied, and her already packed night looked fit to burst in a shower of red and purple glitter.

"Fine, but I am so telling Mom and Dad about your glitter stash."

Ellen followed the six Risakos into the living room and shuddered. The glitter situation had gotten worse. The sofa practically glowed purple, and slashes of red twinkled on the walls, clashing with the dusky orange of the paint. She had no idea how she was going to get this mess cleaned up before Mom and Dad got home.

Annoyance flared in her chest. She'd barely even signed up

to babysit one Little Sister, but somehow she'd ended up with six irritating little scientists, all of whom were trying to explain their plight to her at the same time. It sounded like a squabble between the blue jays that sometimes built nests in the backyard.

"Be quiet, all of you," Ellen said. "I don't care how your machine malfunctioned. My jobs tonight are to get my homework and chores done, give you dinner, and keep you out of trouble. Unraveling your crazy science experiments is not on that list. I thought I told you...uh, three of you, anyway...to clean all this glitter up."

Three of the Risakos looked sheepish, while the other three just looked bored.

"We were going to clean it up, but we couldn't decide who should be in charge," said one of the three that Ellen assumed were the first batch she'd arrived home to.

"The original Risako ought to be in charge," said another.

The first one crossed her arms, sending a shower of glitter to the carpet. Ellen cringed.

"Yes, we all agreed on that, but we couldn't decide who the original was."

"The original is the one who first used the multiplier machine!" said the third Risako.

"We've been over this, we all remember doing that. So we figured that only the original would be able to make any more copies."

Ellen's head spun as she worked to keep up with the conversation, but she thought she understood what had happened. "You each made a copy of yourself, right? If you thought the original was the only one who could make a copy, why didn't you stop after the first one?"

All three "original" Little Sisters blinked at her like a clutch of baby owls.

"That's not how you do science," the middle one finally said.

Ellen ignored the condescending tone and the sage nodding of the other two. She had to turn to more practical matters, such as the way the three definite copies were wandering off.

"Hey, you three, don't you dare leave while this mess is still here," she shouted after them.

They all looked back over their shoulders, and one of them shrugged. "We didn't make that mess. It's not our problem."

"Yeah, I'm not responsible."

"I'm going to go work on the rocket ship."

One of the three "original" Little Sisters stomped her foot. "Hey, that's not fair! I made copies so *they* could do the boring work while I got to mess with the rocket ship."

Ellen stared at her. "Risako! That's very selfish of you. If you ask someone for help, you have to take on your fair share of the work, too. Besides, aren't you the one who has to have read the books when you get to class tomorrow, anyway?"

Risako pouted at the floor and slumped her sparkly shoulders. "I know. But reading is so...boring."

Ellen frowned. Risako had seemed like she was going to say a different word, but had changed her mind at the last moment. When Ellen looked at the other two "originals" for clarification, they simply shrugged.

"Definitely boring," one said.

"Super boring," the other quipped.

Ellen rolled her eyes. She'd take a good book over complicated equations any day.

But she didn't have time for reading tonight, and the scientists didn't have time for rocket ships, no matter how many copies they made of themselves.

A shiver went through Ellen at the thought of any more Risakos appearing tonight. The realization that she had to wrangle six Little Sisters was finally settling over her, weighing her down more effectively than her laden backpack had this afternoon. She couldn't handle any more stress tonight; there was just too much to do and nowhere near enough time.

And then a loud boom sounded from the backyard. Framed pictures rattled against the walls, and little showers of glitter rained onto the carpet. The odor of burning paper floated from the back door.

The three "originals" jumped and screeched, but Ellen just groaned. She didn't have to be good at math to realize that one Ellen didn't have good odds versus six Little Sisters.

Another boom shook the house, sending the three "originals" running for the back door. Ellen followed hot on their heels. At least if she kept as many Little Sisters in sight as possible, she might have a chance of stopping mischief before it started—or rather, before it got worse!

A layer of glitter had settled over the driveway, and where Little Sister's cardboard rocket ship had once sat alone beside the garage, two perfect—but glittery—copies joined it.

The three Little Sisters who were definitely copies surveyed their work as Ellen and the three "originals" emerged from the house.

"They're wasting all the glitter by copying such a big object. How did they get hold of the copy machine?" asked the Little Sister to Ellen's right, scowling. "I thought you had it."

The one on Ellen's left grimaced. "I put it down when Ellen was talking to us. I thought she'd get mad if she thought we weren't all paying attention."

"Don't make this my fault," Ellen grumbled. She deliberately turned her attention from the "originals" and focused on the copies. "I thought you guys were going to improve the rocket ship, not use the copier on it," she yelled.

The three Risako copies shrugged as one, and the middle one answered her. "We couldn't agree on who got to work on what part, so we just made copies so we can each do everything ourselves."

Ellen bit back a scream. Why did every version of Little Sister think copying things would solve every problem that came up tonight? "None of you can play with the rocket ship until the living room is cleaned up and we've had dinner."

But the three copies ignored her, each moving to one of the three rocket ships without squabbling. The three "originals" watched with their mouths open, looking like baby owls once again.

The "original" on the right rounded on the other two. "Why didn't we think of that?"

"Because someone has to do the homework!" said the middle one, stomping her foot.

Yes, the homework, Ellen thought, her heart threatening to plummet to her feet again. She still had to somehow get her math homework done on top of all of Little Sister's uncooperative shenanigans.

"Let's focus on the cleanup and dinner first," Ellen said. "We can all sit together at the table and work on our homework after that."

The Little Sister working on the closest rocket ship looked up from reattaching the rear thrusters. "We could make more rocket ships for each of you, too."

All three "originals" bit their lips, as if the words of agreement hovered just behind.

Exasperation swept through Ellen in a rush. Glitter swirled in eddies around her feet as she stomped over to the three rocket ships, crossed her arms over her chest, and utilized her best, most intimidating imitation of Mom.

"That is *it*! Mom and Dad left me in charge tonight, and that means we do what I say. None of you are allowed to work on your rocket ships, or any other science experiments, until we finish my list of chores. Any Risako who doesn't cooperate will be *told on*!"

Six gasps echoed like surround sound as Ellen's threat sank in. When no other reply followed, Ellen continued. "It's getting late, since you all have wasted a lot of time making copies instead of actually doing your work, so we'll have dinner now and then clean up afterwards."

She turned on her heel, making no commands for the Little Sisters to follow her. Her threat would keep them in line at least long enough to get them started on dinner. Ellen just hoped full tummies would extend the effect.

Sure enough, a line of obedient Little Sisters shuffled into the kitchen behind Ellen. They kept quiet as they climbed into the chairs around the Western-style dinner table, letting the creaky wood speak their dejection for them. They took up every available chair, and Ellen briefly entertained the idea of bringing out the low Japanese-style table Mom and Dad used for special occasions. But getting the big piece of furniture out and setting it all up would take precious time she didn't have. She and the Little Sisters would just have to cram more chairs around this table.

Ellen opened the refrigerator, letting the rush of cold air soothe her for a moment. She needed to stay calm and collected to deal with Little Sister.

But when she looked at what Mom had left for their dinner, the panic came crashing back over her.

Natto! Why had Mom left *natto* for dinner? She knew Ellen didn't like the sticky, stinky mess of soybeans, and Risako often flat refused to eat the stuff.

Ellen glanced over her shoulder and found the Little Sisters bickering together about rocket ship parts. None of them had noticed the vile dinner that awaited them.

With one hand, Ellen swung the refrigerator door closed, and with the other she opened the cabinet and pulled the rice cooker out. Maybe she could make this work with enough rice. She'd have to make a ton of rice anyway, with so many more Risakos to feed than Mom had anticipated. The natto was enough to serve as pure torture to two girls, but split amongst seven, it might be easier to stomach.

Luckily Mom often hosted parties with other Japanese ladies in the area, so her rice cooker was large enough to handle feeding a crowd.

Ellen measured out three cups of rice, hoping that would be enough. Mom might get mad at wasted food, but Ellen would rather have enough to satisfy her multiplied sibling than too little. The hiss of the rice against the metal bowl of the rice cooker covered the argument going on at the table.

"Are you making rice? But I wanted to eat udon tonight."

Ellen paused, her finger hovering over the rice cooker's button. Was Little Sister really going to pull this trick on her tonight? "Risako..."

"What about cold soba noodles?" another Little Sister suggested.

"Ramen! With pork and a hard-boiled egg!"

"Why can't we ever have cheeseburgers for dinner? Mom always makes Japanese stuff."

"Cheeseburgers, cheeseburgers!"

Ellen gritted her teeth together and pushed the button hard enough to make the rice cooker screech against the countertop. "Everyone be quiet. Mom left stuff for us to have for dinner, so that's what we're having. I don't have time to make enough cheeseburgers for all of you, anyway."

"You could make just one and use the copy machine on it," said one Little Sister in the most reasonable tone of voice Ellen had heard from any of them all evening.

"No way," Ellen said. "One, I wouldn't use that thing on food. Who wants to eat glitter? And two, you can't keep making copies of things like this. It's not a good way to solve problems."

She pulled plates out of the cabinets, handling their weight two at a time so she wouldn't drop them. Bad enough she'd have to explain why she'd dirtied so many dishes, she didn't want to add broken plates on top of everything else.

Of course, "everything else" included the fact that her homework still sat uncompleted on the kitchen table, right in the middle of all the Little Sisters. Surely *they* wouldn't have much trouble with it, even if it was sixth-grade math. Little Sister was smart, and six Little Sisters working together could figure out any problem, as they were discovering now via their combined efforts to come up with improved schematics for the rocket ship.

Ellen scowled. If only she could get them to cooperate like that on something useful, her night would become loads easier.

While the rice cooked, she rearranged the chairs to make room for another at a corner of the table. Then, once the rice was ready, Ellen worked to dish up seven servings. She snuck even portions of the *natto* under each heaping mound, then poured a generous spread of soy sauce over them.

To Risako's credit, each one of her thanked Ellen as she sat their plates before them. They even waited to start eating until Ellen sat down with her own helping.

"*Itadakimasu!*" they all said.

Ellen mumbled her own thanks for the food along with the chorus, but now that the hoard of doppelgangers was occupied, her mind couldn't avoid the pit of despair that was forming around her math homework. Distracted, she shoved a bite of rice into her mouth.

Huh, she thought. *The* natto *isn't so bad all together with the rice and soy sauce.* She took another bite. The Little Sisters didn't seem to realize their rice hid anything undesirable, either. Maybe once dinner was over, the six of them would stay calm enough to help Ellen clean up, and then she'd manage to get a moment to give her homework another real try.

Then the next explosion from the backyard rocked the house.

When the ringing in her ears quieted down, Ellen found herself alone in the kitchen with a dining table full of dirty dishes. Didn't that just figure? Washing all of these by herself would take a good half hour at least. She glanced at the clock over the stove and grimaced. Mom and Dad might be home by then!

But she couldn't start on any of the kitchen cleanup yet, not until this glitter mess was dealt with. Not to mention clearing away whatever new mayhem had begun outside now!

Her chair squeaked against the kitchen tile when she pushed away from the table and stood. If she'd thought the weight of responsibility had affected her posture earlier in the evening, the slump of her shoulders now would probably have a doctor diagnosing an oncoming deformity.

Resigned, she trudged towards the back door. A sense of dread trickled through her heart the closer she got to it. When she finally opened the door and saw what the Little Sisters were up to, she felt like someone had reached into her chest and squeezed her lungs until all the air was gone.

The number of rocket ships on the driveway had returned

to one, but the amount of glitter had increased so much that Ellen could barely make out the driveway underneath the carpet of purple and red sparkles. The Little Sisters were all knelt down in the mess, picking up handfuls of the stuff and letting it sift back down between their fingers while they *hmm*'ed and murmured their hypotheses to one another.

Overhead, the sky sported bands of pink and purple, and the sun inched ever closer to the roofs of their western neighbor's houses. The intermittent chirps of crickets rose from the bushes.

One of the Little Sisters stood up, not bothering to brush the glitter from her knees. Ellen thought she was one of the originals, but she couldn't really tell anymore.

"I've finished my preliminary investigation into the cause of the glitter bomb-ination of the two rocket ships. It is clear to me that the remaining ship is the original one, based on the residue of matcha powder inside the fuel tank from the trip to Mars. This indicates that the copies were unstable."

Another Risako piped up. "What does that mean for us? Are we unstable, too?"

"Ugh, I don't want to turn into a glitter bomb," said another.

Little Sister number four looked up from the copy machine she held. "No, we copies won't explode. My data shows the malfunction in the ship copies was introduced due to them being made when the copy machine was almost out of glitter, and now the machine is broken. We pushed it too hard. It was only a prototype, after all."

"Well, that's a relief."

"Now that there's only one ship left, we can all work together to tune up the parts we discussed at dinner!" said the first Risako. Her declaration elicited cheers of agreement from the other five.

Finally, Ellen managed to work some air back into her lungs.

"*No!*" she yelled. The echo of it bouncing off the garage door surprised her, but she didn't let her surprise steal her newfound wind. She was done letting Little Sister walk all over her tonight.

Now all six Little Sisters looked at her, their mouths hanging open and the glitter in their hair sparking in the deepening sunset.

"Mom and Dad will be home once it gets dark, and nothing has been accomplished except for a little dinner. I haven't been able to do my homework. You guys haven't even tried to do your reading, and instead you've made a glitter minefield out of the backyard and the living room. The kitchen is a mess, too. You know what Mom will say if she finds out we didn't do the dishes after dinner."

One of the Little Sisters gulped.

Ellen nodded. "That's right. We'll both—uh, all—be grounded if she sees any of this mess. That means no rocket ship for anyone." *And no* Neko-Hime *for me*, she thought sadly. After this disaster, it might be *years* before Ellen got to find out what happened next in her favorite manga series.

The version of Risako who had declared the copy machine to be broken shoved the useless device into her skirt pocket. "We'll help you clean up, Ellen. Just tell us what to do."

The rest of the Little Sisters nodded their agreement.

Ellen pulled her shoulders back. She had no time to waste wrestling with her growing sense of defeat. "Okay, we'll split into three groups, two Risakos to each group. You two," she pointed at the two standing on the left, "will stay out here and use the hose to wash the glitter on the driveway into the gutter. You two in the middle will vacuum up the living room, and the last two will come help me wash the dishes. Got it?"

The Little Sisters saluted as one and hopped to their

assigned chores like soldiers whose drill sergeant marched a mere pace behind them. Team Hose had the garden hose uncoiled across the lawn by the time Ellen stepped inside the house, and the squeak of the spigot and the rush of the water outside gave way to the high-pitched roar of Team Vacuum starting up in the living room.

The two Little Sisters Ellen had assigned to Team Kitchen followed behind her.

"What should we do?" asked the one on the right.

"I'll make the soapy water," Ellen said. "You guys bring the dishes over for me to wash, then one of you will dry, and the other will put the dishes away."

The Little Sisters followed her directions, and the three of them worked together as quickly as they dared to put the dishes and the kitchen aright.

Soapy water splattered all over Ellen's arms as she wiped and scrubbed each dish with vigor. From the living room, exclamations of "over here" and "there's some more" punctuated the continuing vacuum sounds. Through the window over the sink Ellen caught glimpses of those two Risakos running the hose back and forth, driving the waves of glitter farther down the driveway.

Still, over all the noise, Ellen swore she heard the ticking of the clock the loudest.

"Where's the next dish," she panted, dragging the back of her wrist across her forehead.

"That was the last one," said one of the Little Sisters. "And I got the chairs put back where they belong."

Ellen looked around. Sure enough, the kitchen shone. Maybe it wasn't as spotless as Mom could make it, but it certainly wouldn't get them grounded. Unable to help herself, she glanced at the clock. Fifteen minutes remained until Mom and Dad came home.

"Good job, guys," Ellen said. She let herself release a tiny sigh of relief as she pulled the plug in the drain. By the time the water finished glugging down the disposal, the whine of the vacuum had cut off, too.

Ellen gave her hands a few brisk wipes with the damp towel before going to check on Team Vacuum.

One Little Sister was shoving the cushions back onto the couch while the other coiled the power cord around the back of the vacuum. Ellen scanned the carpet, looked under the furniture and along the floorboards, but couldn't find a speck of anything that sparkled.

"Wow, this looks great," she said. She grabbed Mom's decorative throw pillows and put them back on the couch with a reverent pat. "Mom won't even notice a difference."

The back door squealed open, and a moment later the last two Risakos entered the living room. Ellen gave silent thanks that they had remembered to change out of their most likely soaked and glitter-encrusted outside shoes and into some house slippers. One of them wore Dad's huge pair, and they flopped around her feet like a diver's fins.

"We did our best. I don't think even Dad will find a speck of glitter out there."

"Yeah, we washed it all down the storm drain out front of the neighbors' house."

Ellen put her hands on her hips. "Did you remember to turn the water off and wrap the hose back up by the spigot?"

Both Little Sisters rolled their eyes. "Duh."

"Okay, great," Ellen said quickly. No need to start an argument in the home stretch. "I'm proud of all of you guys. We really came together and got the place cleaned up." She tactfully didn't mention again how the whole mess was Risako's fault in the first place, but the way all six of them kicked at the freshly vacuumed carpet told her they realized the truth of the matter.

Only two problems remained to take care of before Mom and Dad got home. Neither of them had finished their homework, and...

"They're gonna be really mad if they find six of us Risakos here, aren't they?" said the Risako at Ellen's elbow.

"Probably more mad about that than the fact neither of us have done our homework," Ellen said. "Do you guys really have no idea who the real original Risako is?"

The Little Sisters looked at one another, biting their lips and shrugging. "Not really."

Ellen tapped her finger against her cheek, thinking. "Well, do any of you know what you planned to do when the copies weren't needed any longer?"

A Little Sister beside the couch nodded. "I built a 'consolidate' function into the prototype copier, and meant to use it to collapse all of us into one again once my copies had finished reading those books. But," she pulled the broken copy machine from her pocket and frowned at it, "that won't work anymore."

"Does that plan sound familiar to anyone else?" Ellen asked.

The remaining Risakos all nodded, and Ellen thought hard to come up with some other tidbit that only the original Little Sister might know. One of their past adventures sprang to mind. "What dinosaur did I save you from when we fought over your time machine?"

One Risako crossed her arms. "We didn't fight over it, you tried to steal it from me!"

"And I hardly think rescuing me from either the T. Rex or the pterodactyl counts when it was all your fault to begin with," said another. The rest added their agreements.

Ellen fought a grimace and tried another memory. "Well then, what treasure did I pull up during our expedition to the sea floor?"

The Risako sitting on the couch rolled her eyes. "It was just a lame action figure."

"At least some gold doubloons would have funded my research for another year. Why didn't you grab any of those?" asked another.

Ellen put a hand on her forehead. A little voice inside her that sounded a lot like her math teacher told her she was making this equation too complicated.

Well, she thought, *if one Risako equals another, then any Risako will do just as well as any other.* If they couldn't even tell the difference between themselves, how should Ellen or their parents be expected to?

Ellen put a hand on the nearest Little Sister's shoulder. "Since I'm still in charge here, I say you are my Little Sister."

The selected Risako shrugged. "Works for me."

The others shrugged as well, all apparently in agreement.

With the decision made, Ellen let her relief spread through her. She wished she had a sticker to slap across Risako's forehead. She needed to make sure she kept track of her until they got the copies sorted.

"That's great and all, but what are we going to do about Mom and Dad finding out about the rest of us?" asked one of the copies.

"Yeah, I don't want to be grounded just for existing," grumbled another.

Ellen nodded. "Don't worry, I have an idea. Let's all go out to the rocket ship."

The last rays of sunlight streamed over the neighbors' roofs, and the crickets were in full swing on tonight's performance. The last few puddles on the driveway were shrinking, leaving clean concrete behind.

The Little Sisters huddled around Ellen where she stood beside the rocket ship. Risako, the one Ellen had declared as the real one, waited a little closer to the house so they wouldn't get her mixed up with the others again.

"I'm sending the five of you into space to do important research," Ellen announced.

Five wide grins appeared on their faces, but Risako made a sound of protest.

Ellen held up a finger. "The copies can do more research than you could by yourself, and they'll share their findings with you using the radio in the rocket ship. You'll all get to increase your knowledge of the universe by working together. It won't be an easy job. Science is very serious, you know."

"We can do it!"

"We'll work hard!"

"But...but my rocket ship!"

"Think of it as an excuse to build a better one from the ground up," Ellen said. "*After* you finish your homework."

With the moment of Mom and Dad's arrival approaching at near light speed, Ellen shepherded all the copies into the rocket ship and closed the door. "You have enough green stuff in the fuel tank, right?"

"Yep, it's all full of grass clippings from the last time Dad mowed."

"Okay then, steer carefully. Watch out for the Moon, it really sneaks up on you. Risako will be waiting for your first report!"

Ellen patted the top of the rocket ship, then went to stand with Risako by the back door. They held hands and watched the copies lift off.

Risako sighed. "I'm really sorry I made things so hard for

you tonight, Ellen. I really only meant to help you with the copies."

Ellen squeezed her hand. "I understand, and thanks for the sentiment, but neither of us will learn the hard stuff if we have someone else do the work for us."

"I know. And reading really is...hard. It's hard, and that's kind of embarrassing." Risako swallowed, her face downcast.

Ellen knelt down and pulled her into a hug. "I totally get being embarrassed about having a harder time with one subject when you're so good at another. How about we both promise to work hard and encourage one another?"

Risako nodded and hugged Ellen back.

They went back inside just as Mom and Dad's cars pulled up to the driveway. In silent agreement, the two of them waited in the living room for their parents to come in.

Mom wore the same pinched expression as she had last week after Ellen's parent-teacher conference. Dad didn't look happy, either.

"Risako, your teacher says you haven't been doing your reading homework! I'm very disappointed in you," said Mom.

Risako looked at her feet. "I'm sorry."

"I expect you to take your books upstairs right now and get started," said Dad. "There will be no science experiments until you can show us that you've done your reading homework every day this week."

Risako nodded and bent to pick up her books from where they'd fallen off the couch.

A sparkle of glitter glimmered from beneath them, and both Ellen and Risako stiffened.

Mom let out a strangled sound. "Is that *glitter?!*"

Ellen stepped in. "It's my fault, Mom. I thought I'd give her some to keep her occupied so I could get my homework done, but it ended up making a huge mess, even though we tried really hard to clean it up. I...I didn't get my homework done tonight, either."

That last part came out quiet, and Ellen couldn't help hanging her head as she said it.

Mom sighed. "Risako, please take your books upstairs. Your father will check on you in a little while."

Risako scampered away, books clutched to her chest, but she shot a grateful look over her shoulder at Ellen before she disappeared up the stairs.

Ellen chewed her lip. She would accept her punishment and work even harder tomorrow.

Mom sat on the couch and patted the cushion beside her.

Ellen sat down and wiped at her eyes.

"It's okay, Ellen. You're not in trouble."

"I'm not?" Ellen said. It ended on a hiccup, but she didn't care.

Mom shook her head. "Dad and I have seen how hard you've been trying all week, and I know Risako can be a little hard to manage sometimes."

Ellen almost laughed. Mom didn't even know the half of it. Or, more accurately, she didn't know the sixth of it. *Maybe I'm starting to understand fractions a little better.*

Still, she couldn't keep banging her head against a mathematical wall. "I think I'm going to ask for a math tutor at school tomorrow," she said.

"That's a smart idea, honey," Mom said. "There's no shame in asking for help when you need it. In fact, I think Risako might need a tutor, too. I don't suppose you'd be willing to help your sister with her reading, would you?"

Ellen smiled. "Sure, I can do that."

She knew she could make the lessons fun, and maybe even get Little Sister hooked on *Neko-Hime* along the way. Surely

Risako would have something to say on the scientific possibilities of the shape-shifting princess.

But for herself, Ellen would stick with a school-assigned tutor. She needed only a normal understanding of math, not her sister's mad scientist schemes!

About the Author

Brigid Collins is a fantasy and science fiction writer living in Nevada. Her fantasy series *The Songbird River Chronicles, Winter's Consort,* and *The Clockwork Kingdom Saga,* as well as her dark fairy tale novella *Thorn and Thimble* are available wherever books are sold. Her short stories have appeared in *Fiction River, Feyland Tales,* and Mercedes Lackey's *Valdemar* anthologies.

Want an extra Sugimori Sisters story? Sign up for her newsletter at www.brigidcollinsbooks.com/newsletter-sign-up/ and get a free copy of *Strength & Chaos, Mischief & Poise: Four Cat Tales,* exclusively available to her subscribers!

~

Support Brigid on Patreon! Featuring monthly short stories, blog posts, and behind-the-scenes tidbits in a pay-what-you-want structure. Come hang out! patreon.com/BrigidCollins